late
fall

late
fall

noelle adams

BRAIN MILL PRESS · GREEN BAY, WISCONSIN

Published in the United States by Brain Mill Press.
A Brain Mill Press fine first edition.
STANDARD PRINT ISBN 978-1-942083-26-9
EPUB ISBN 978-1-942083-27-6
MOBI ISBN 978-1-942083-28-3
PDF ISBN 978-1-942083-29-0

Cover photograph © Jan Rios.
Cover design by Monika MacFarlane.
Interior design by Williams Writing, Editing & Design.

Interested in reading more from Brain Mill Press?
Join our mailing list at www.brainmillpress.com.

contents

late
fall

one

*A*lmost every morning for the last twenty-five years, I've walked a dirt path that leads from my backyard to a little graveyard in the woods.

On this, my last morning, I do it one more time.

It's not as easy as it sounds, although the walk is less than half a mile. I have to take my walker, which I hate even the sight of, and I have to rest several times along the way.

My hip surgery was just a few weeks ago, and walking still isn't easy. My doctor says it may never be easy again, but that's a depressing thought I refuse to believe.

Everyone tells me that positive thinking is particularly important at my stage of life. This is a ridiculous claim, as anyone knows who has ever tried to use positive thinking as a tool. The world doesn't change because you want it to. Your body doesn't feel better because you talk yourself into believing it. We tell ourselves these lies because we want to feel as though we have some sort of control over what happens to us—even those things that are completely out of our hands. So we pretend our conscious thoughts are more powerful than anything else because we want so much for them to be so.

1

I know better. Positive thinking isn't the miracle cure that we want it to be. My sister continued thinking the best on each of the 461 days she fought against cancer.

The cancer took her anyway.

But I still hope every evening that I'll walk a little easier the following day. I keep hoping because I'm a human being, and that's what we do. We *hope,* whether or not reality can ever answer those hopes.

This morning, the pain in my hip, my back, even my legs is a little worse than it was yesterday—I assume because I'm trying to decrease my pain medication so I don't fall asleep every time I sit down.

I have to make the walk to the graveyard today, though. It's my last morning. It's my last chance to say good-bye.

It's the end of August, one of those last hot, humid days that summer throws at us in defiance, even as it's on its way out. Not even seven in the morning yet, and I still feel a trickle of sweat run down my breastbone as I lift my walker over a tree root.

I pause for a minute to catch my breath and consider sitting down in the little seat on my walker to rest my legs. But I'm afraid if I sit down it will be too hard to get up, so instead I push on.

I used to hike nearly every weekend. When I was forty, Jeff and I hiked the Appalachian Trail over the summer, starting in our county in southwest Virginia and making it all the way up to New York.

We always talked about doing the entire trail, but we couldn't get that much time off from work, and we split up a few years later anyway.

I ache to be forty again, with strong legs and hiking boots and hair that hung all the way down my back, stepping out onto an outcropping where I could see miles of summer slopes and valleys, believing that at my side was the man with whom I'd spend the rest of my life.

I was with Jeff for eight years, longer than I was with anyone else. But he'd always wanted kids, and at forty-two, it was now-or-never-time for me, and I just didn't want that life.

He found a pretty woman in her thirties to marry, and they have three boys and eight grandkids now.

It's a different life than the one I've led—one of those movie reels of could-have-been that run through my head from time to time. The colors are vivid and the soundtrack is happy, but the woman playing that domestic part just isn't *me*.

So I'll be seventy-two years old next March, and I'm alone. Never been married. Never had a child. My one sister and my parents are long dead.

I've never really been lonely, though. I've never quite understood what loneliness is. After all, I always had my friends and my books and the company of my own thoughts. And, until two months ago, I always had a dog.

That last thought is not one I should let myself

dwell on—not when I still have to make it up the last little hill as the path curves upward to the graveyard.

I clear my mind and ignore the pain because it's so important that I make it all the way this morning. When the curve around the slight slope evens out, I can see the sunny clearing broken by eight stone markers, one for each grave.

People trace their lives in different ways. Many do it by stages of their family—engaged, newlywed, one child, two children, empty nest, grandchildren. Others do it by places they've lived or the various positions they've held during their careers.

I've always traced the lines of my life by my dogs.

As I finally reach the small graveyard, it's as though I can see the years of my life spread out before me in the eight stones—just big rocks I found on the property—that identify where I buried each of my dogs.

The first was Austen, the sweet springer spaniel I adopted when I got my first job after graduating college. Austen was exuberant until the day she died, giving my twenties a happiness they might not otherwise have possessed. I hated the secretarial job I had then, I was always struggling with money because I didn't want to rely on my parents, and I was endlessly frustrated romantically, since the men I was interested in never gave me a second glance.

After Austen died, I made the decision to go to graduate school in library science, and I had two dogs in my thirties as I was finally diving into a career I loved as a college librarian. Both dogs were springer spaniels like Austen. Brontë died too early from liver failure, and O'Connor, who was never without her tennis ball, hadn't been strong enough to hike the Appalachian Trail with Jeff and me.

O'Connor died shortly before I broke up with Jeff and was replaced by Shelley, a black cocker spaniel. Shelley was quiet and loved to cuddle up with me as I read, and I'd needed that in my midforties. Her soft, warm body was a comfort, always waiting for me with a wagging tail when I came home from work. I continued to move up in position at the library, until Shelley died about the time I became the director of the library for the same private liberal arts college I'd attended as an undergraduate.

I got another cocker spaniel after Shelley. Rossetti was plagued with health problems, but she had the sweetest, most patient spirit. I spent a lot of time and money taking care of her. It made me worried about getting another cocker spaniel, since the breed is prone to such problems. I had to have a knee replaced in my midfifties, and I decided to change to a smaller dog. Eliot and Browning were both King Charles spaniels. They were sisters and I couldn't decide between them or split them up, so I ended up with both. They were small and social and adorable with their smashed-in noses and bright eyes. They saw me through the end of my career.

There was only one dog after that.

I adopted Alcott from a shelter. She was a brown cocker spaniel who came to me with only one eye. She was my companion in retirement, until she died of cancer two months ago.

I was going to get a new dog last month, but then I fell and had to have surgery.

So there was no dog after Alcott. I'm not even sure I want one. Losing them gets harder and harder.

But I've always understood myself as a woman with a dog. It's been part of my identity for as long as I can remember.

I'm not sure who I am now that Alcott is dead. She was my last dog. She'll have to be. Today is my last day, and I can't have a dog anymore.

I stare down at the large, lopsided rock my nephew helped me drag over after we buried Alcott, and I miss her so much I feel the pain surging up through my chest, my throat, my eyes.

I've never been one to cry in public, but I used to cry on my own, when no one else could see. After menopause, however, I've cried less and less, like my tears have simply dried up.

I cry now, though, thinking of Alcott's eyes as the veterinarian put her to sleep not so many weeks ago, the little tail that wagged weakly even at the end.

And then I'm crying for all of them—all eight stones, the eight dogs who have marked the years of my life.

Or maybe I'm just crying for myself, because I have to say good-bye today.

I lived on these two acres in the mountains of southwest Virginia during my childhood and then again for the last twenty-five years. My mother was born here. She inherited it from her parents, and she passed it on to me when she died. She never explained why she willed the property to me and not my sister, but I always assumed it was because my sister had a child.

My mother loved me and was proud of me all her life, but she always believed there was a hole in my life because I didn't have a husband or family of my own.

My mother died around the time I broke up with Jeff, so I moved out here then and commuted the thirty minutes into town for my job. The house is more than a hundred years old—just a two-bedroom farmhouse in constant need of work and repair. I've loved it, though. The living room window looks into Valentine Valley, and the view has been another of my constant companions.

I can't begin to calculate the amount of money I've poured into this house and land since I've owned them, and I've finally had to acknowledge that I simply can't keep them up. I have a decent retirement income, but I have no idea how long I'll live, so I can't dump it all into renovating this house.

Plus, I no longer have the energy to do the daily

upkeep. I can usually take care of myself fine, but the household chores that should be simple are taking nearly all of my daytime hours, since I have to do them so slowly now.

It's not like I'm in particularly bad shape. I have some arthritis, and I have digestive problems when I eat onions, berries, nuts, or red meat. I pee a little in my pants whenever I sneeze or laugh, but there has been nothing truly debilitating about my health until recently.

My nephew, Roger, was particularly concerned after I fell in the bathroom last month and broke my hip. I couldn't reach the phone, and it was an hour before my neighbor dropped by for a chat and a cup of tea. Roger said he didn't think I should live alone anymore, and I can't even say he was wrong.

So the house and land are going to him—he's paid a fair market price for it, and there's no worry of his taking advantage—and I'm going to an assisted-living home.

I thought I was resigned to this reality. I no longer have the energy for angst the way I did when I was younger. Raving against what feels like injustice doesn't accomplish anything except using up our emotional resources, so I don't do it anymore.

This is life. After summer, the green leaves always change colors and fall off the trees. Dogs die, no matter how much you love them. Land is sold, even if you used to tell yourself you were going to die on the property. And people get old.

Even me.

So this morning I have to say a final good-bye to my dogs and become an old woman who doesn't have one. I have to leave these acres with their lush green lawns and thick woods that slope halfway up the mountain. I have to become someone living in a retirement home with a lot of old people I don't know.

I'm tired anyway. I can do the clichéd thing and tell myself I've had a good life. I don't need to hope for anything anymore, and maybe there's a kind of respite in that.

Maybe.

I don't know if you've ever tried it, but telling yourself there's nothing to hope for doesn't ever work.

We're human beings, after all, and *hope* is what we do.

A half hour later, I make it back to the house, where Beth, my grandniece, is sweeping out the kitchen.

I've always been neat and organized, so when we cleared it out last week, my house wasn't filled with piles of clutter and mementos from previous decades like a lot of my friends' have been. But the house is mostly empty now, except the few family antiques that I've given to my nephew.

"How are you feeling, Aunt Ellie?" Beth asks, ducking her head out of the kitchen as I shuffle in with my walker.

"Just fine." My full name is Eleanor, but for as long as I can remember, everyone has always called me Ellie.

I see Beth studying me, and I know she's looking for signs that I'm going to fall down or pass out or something.

Beth is my nephew's youngest child, and she's a good-natured, rather bohemian girl in her twenties with long brown hair like I used to have. As a teenager, Beth would come and visit me at the house quite often, painting the landscape or watching the birds and squirrels. In typical adolescent fashion, some of her interest was an act—an attempt to play out an artistic role as she understood it—but I've always enjoyed her company, and she has always been welcome.

"I'm a little tired," I admit, mostly so she can feel her concern is validated. "But I'll just rest a few minutes before we leave."

"Of course," Beth says with a wide smile. "We can take all the time you want."

You get used to those looks after a while—after your hair turns gray and your body starts to ache in ways it never did before. Those looks from younger people that try just a little too hard to treat you like normal. It has nothing to do with their not loving you or wanting what's best for you. It has more to do with their genuinely believing you're different from them.

I used to resent it when people would give me that look of condescending, exaggerated cheer.

Now, it happens too often to even care anymore.

"Would you like a cup of tea before we leave?" Beth asks, leaning the broom against the wall in a way that is obviously unbalanced.

The broom falls over with a loud clatter, causing Beth to give a little jump.

I don't even blink. "That would be lovely. Thank you."

When I was twenty-five, I made a trip to England with two of my friends, and I came back with a passion for tea. Part of it was probably for show—a young woman's desire to appear classy and cosmopolitan amid all the American coffee drinkers—but I was so committed to tea-drinking that it soon became a real part of my life.

I sit down now in an antique rocking chair—one that's too uncomfortable to ever use for long—in front of the expansive front window in the living room. I sip the tea that Beth brings me and stare out at the view of Valentine Valley.

The trees are still green, so the variation in the

landscape is minimal, the bright green of the grass melting into the dark and lighter greens of the trees as the mountains curve down into a distinctive bowl shape, with one side that cuts jaggedly down into a ravine as the river breaks through.

No one in the county agrees on how Valentine Valley got its name. Some say that the ravine cutting that way makes the shape of the valley look vaguely like a heart. There's also an old wives' tale that is still occasionally told about a farmer who took his bride to this valley on Valentine's Day, where she said they had to stop and build their house.

I don't really believe the story. Most places are named after people, so I assume there was a Mr. Valentine who settled in this area centuries ago.

It doesn't matter. I love the valley, however it got its name.

There was fog earlier this morning, and there are still wisps of it floating around the edges of the rounded mountain peaks, casting an almost ghostly aura on the light and shadow of the landscape, shrouding the off-centered heart of the valley in mist.

In my early fifties, I dated a photographer for several months, and he took a whole series of photos of the valley, which ended up doing quite well for him and earning him an exhibit at a moderately prestigious gallery. He said that the distinct geography of the scene made it an artist's endless challenge. He said it was nearly impossible to truly capture the look of it. Then he said that I was like the valley—there being something elusive about me that caused men to set out on quests, although they would never really believe I could be won.

Maybe he was trying to impress me, since he knew I loved the valley so much, but I still remember the words and think about them sometimes.

I was always pretty enough—not beautiful or particularly distinctive, but pretty. But I was never one of those popular women for whom men fall all over themselves. It bothered me when I was younger, since I felt like there was something lacking about me, an appeal I was missing but really wanted.

The last man I had any interest in was Carl, whom I met at a church function about eight years ago. We went to the movies and to symphony concerts and to plays at the college together for about a month, until he had a heart attack.

His ex-wife came back to him then, so I was summarily dismissed.

I didn't even mind all that much.

I've been good at a lot of things in my life. I'm good at books and was good at my job and was good with dogs and have always been good at holding onto my friends.

I have never been good with men. While it's nice to think that the reason is because I'm as elusive as that photographer claimed, it's more likely because there's never been anything about me that men particularly wanted.

Not enough to spend the rest of their lives with me, anyway.

It doesn't matter anymore. That part of my life is over, just like so much else.

I'll still have my books—even when I go to my retirement home—so at least I don't have to give up all of myself.

I also don't have to give up Valentine Valley. Because my nephew paid me for the purchase of the house and property, I've ended up with enough money to afford to live at Eagle's Rest.

It's a very nice home in the next county over, on the other side of the valley, right where the ravine breaks in, forming the dip of the heart.

two

There is a two-hundred-year-old oak tree on the eastern edge of our property. When I was nine years old, it was the grandest tree I'd ever seen, and my summer's ambition was to climb up to the top.

It was a good climbing tree, with plenty of sturdy lower branches, so I had no problem getting halfway up. Three branches came together at one spot to form a kind of seat, and I would hang out there for hours that summer, watching the birds and bugs and dreaming of all kinds of adventures.

The top of the tree was very high, with the branches much younger and bendable. Each day, I would climb as high as I could reach, but I would always chicken out before I got to the very top.

All summer and into the autumn I dreamed of reaching the top branch. I imagined myself getting up there and looking over the highest of the trees in the woods. I thought maybe I could even see the shops and restaurants of Roanoke—the largest city of any size in the region—if a mountain didn't get in the way.

So one fall day after school I determined to do it. My sister was reading a book not far away, but I didn't tell her what I was going to do. I never told anyone the ambitions I had. Sharing them would be giving too much away, making me vulnerable in a way I didn't like.

After all, what if I couldn't manage to climb to the top of the tree? Then other people would know that I'd failed.

That afternoon, I reached my little seat about halfway up, and then I kept climbing. There were a couple of stable branches higher up, and I stretched to grab onto one of them and walked myself up the trunk. It took some effort and upper-body strength, but I was able to haul myself up until I was straddling one of the higher branches.

I felt safe there, and I rested a minute, leaning back against the old trunk. The bark was cracked and slightly scratchy, but it smelled familiar, woody, like a good friend. I loved the feeling of safety—of being high in the air but supported by the large trunk and a sturdy branch.

Sometimes I wish I could still climb trees and feel that kind of pride and security again.

I wasn't at the top yet, though, so after a few minutes I held onto the trunk and pulled my feet under myself to stand on the branch. The higher branches were all flexible, so they moved when I held onto them. I grabbed at one and pulled, testing its strength.

It seemed to support my weight, so I used it to

pull myself up, scrabbling with my feet for some purchase on the tree.

I managed to get higher, and then found a branch to pull myself higher still. I wasn't at the top yet, but I was closer. The leaves were sparser up there, and I could see wide stretches of crisp blue sky above.

The big oak—my good friend of many years—didn't feel nearly as secure up there. I could feel the breeze blowing against my hot skin, rustling the leaves and sending my hair into my eyes. For a moment, it felt like it was going to blow me right out of the tree. I was gripping two different branches so tightly my knuckles hurt, but they would move every time I did, so that stability I loved wasn't there.

I was high in the air—higher than anything else on our property—and I couldn't trust these branches to hold me up.

For several minutes, I was paralyzed, about four feet from the very top—willing myself to continue but terrified of letting go of the two branches I gripped. Finally, after a wave of dizziness overtook me, I just gave up.

Instead of reaching up, I stretched one of my feet down until I felt a branch beneath it. Then I began to lower my weight onto it, telling myself that in just a minute I'd reach that good, strong branch again.

I was evidently too heavy for the branch I'd chosen because it buckled as soon as I gave it my weight. This happens occasionally when you climb trees—every kid knows it—but I was so emotionally stretched at that point that I couldn't react quickly enough to find a new support for my hand or my feet.

I lost my grip and started to slip, falling down against the bark of the tree in a way that tore my shirt and scratched both of my palms and my cheek. I grappled for a branch to hang onto, finding one that broke almost immediately from the momentum of my fall.

Silent panic overtook me, chilling my skin and blurring my vision. I could see myself, in that moment, falling all of the way down the tree, striking against branches and then finally landing with a thud on the ground. I would break my back, break my neck, bust open my skull.

I could see it all, even as my hands kept reaching out for anything strong enough to hold onto.

My fall was stopped abruptly by that nice stable branch I'd been resting on earlier. My foot slipped past it, making me straddle the branch again, catching myself quite painfully with my bottom.

I called all of my private parts "bottom" back then, and the impact was not on the part of my bottom that had extra cushioning. The pain blinded me for a minute, and tears ran down my cheeks as I clung to the trunk and found my balance again.

I was all scratched up, and I'd pulled a couple of muscles in my thighs that ached sharply. Plus the pain from the impact between my legs. But I was stable again. I wasn't falling anymore. I kept telling myself that truth.

I have no idea how long I sat there. It all hurt so much I couldn't climb even if I'd wanted to, but I was too afraid to move again anyway.

I could have called out for help. My sister wasn't that far away, and she would have run over and helped me—or else gone to the house to get assistance from our mother.

I didn't cry out, though. I didn't make a sound. Everything hurt. I couldn't move at all. I was trapped at a significant height in this old oak tree. But everything would be so much worse if I had to ask for help, if I had to admit I couldn't do it on my own.

Eventually, the pain subsided enough for me to risk swinging my leg over the tree. I made it back down to my branch seat, and I felt safe there again. I wiped away my tears and wiped away the blood from my skin. I decided if I was quiet enough I could make it back to the house and into the bathroom without anyone seeing me.

Some people naturally ask for help. They like the attention of having other people run to their rescue. They like leaning on other people for support in their times of need.

I've never understood them. Needing help has always been a very private matter for me. Even as a child, there was something shameful about it. You only accepted help when there was no other choice, and you never, ever asked for it.

I did make it down the tree and back to the house and into the bathroom without my sister or my mother seeing me. I cleaned myself up and verified that nothing was damaged in a way that would be a lasting problem.

I told my mom I'd tripped and fallen down, scratching up my palm and face. I'd already bandaged myself up at that point, so she told me I could have a glass of lemonade if it would make me feel better.

I did have the lemonade. I was shaky for the rest of the day.

The following afternoon, I went back up the tree, but I didn't go any farther than the seat of three branches.

I never tried to climb up to the top of the tree again. Any time I thought about doing it, I'd get a heavy knot in my belly.

I would sometimes dream about getting to the top and looking out at the rooftop of the woods, seeing our house and the old barn, maybe even catching a glimpse of Roanoke in the distance.

I know now that I would never have been able to see that far. With the slope of the land, I probably wouldn't have been able to even see our house. But

I still feel that ache of regret at never reaching the top of the oak.

It's one of those losses that just doesn't go away.

My nephew, Roger, has gone on earlier to my new home, taking my boxes and the few pieces of furniture I'm bringing with me. So it's just Beth who is driving me now as I look back toward the old house, the dilapidated barn, and the much-loved woods and grassy lawns disappearing behind the curve in the road.

"At least it's staying in the family," Beth says, in a voice that's obviously intended to sound cheerful and encouraging.

I appreciate the attempt, no matter how little the tone works. "Yes. I'm very glad your dad wanted it."

"I know it's hard," Beth says, glancing over at my face. "But I think, once you move in, you'll be pleasantly surprised by how nice it is to not have to worry about meals and housekeeping and all that. It's a really nice place."

Eagle's Rest is a nice place. It is *very* nice, as far as assisted-living homes go, and it offers the option of moving to full-time nursing care, should I need it in the future. I visited other, less expensive places, and they made me sick, even just walking in the door.

When I don't answer, Beth goes on. "And it might be nice to have a lot of other people around, at your stage in life. Hopefully, you'll find a lot of friends and things to do. You won't have to be alone."

I smile at her and murmur a wordless answer. I don't want to hurt her feelings. She is a sweet girl, and she is trying to help. But I like being alone. I don't want to be surrounded by a lot of annoying retired people and forced to participate in ridiculous activities I'm expected to enjoy just because I have gray hair.

I didn't like games and ice cream socials when I was younger, and I sure don't want to put up with them now.

I want my books and a view of the Valentine Valley. I'll be okay if I'm left alone with those.

Beth is going on, listing all the good things she can brainstorm about my change in living situation. "And it will be such a relief to know that there's always help if you need it—nurses and assistants and anything you need."

"Yes," I say. "That will be nice."

If I hadn't fallen two months ago, I wouldn't be moving now. Sometimes I curse myself for the one step, the one slip of my foot that caused me to fall and break my hip.

One moment of time, and everything changes. That's always the way it happens, but it doesn't get any easier just because you know it always happens that way.

"And Dad and I will come visit you as often as we can. You know that, right? And I'm sure you can come out to visit the house sometimes too."

"That would be lovely." I'm saying these things because it's expected, because I don't want to hurt her feelings. It would be nice if she'd just drive in silence, but people often aren't comfortable without words, not when things are hard.

So Beth keeps saying encouraging things and I keep acting like I'm encouraged until we finally make it to the other side of the valley and she drives up the mountain to the collection of buildings that make up Eagle's Rest.

There are two large buildings—the main residence with the apartments and dining room, and the community building with lounge spaces, exercise rooms, a swimming pool, and health services. There are also quite a few cottages around the perimeter that are rented out to seniors who want an "independent living" situation, and there are tennis courts and a garden.

It's a gray, humid day, and there aren't very many people outside as Beth parks in one of the visitors' spaces in the front. To the right of the main building, a wide lawn slopes down into woods. There's a path that skirts the woods, leading to a valley overlook.

I know it's there because that path is the reason I chose to spend the rest of my life in Eagle's Rest.

As we reach the front door of the main building, I'm about to pull it open when a middle-aged man walks out.

He blinks in surprise, evidently not having noticed our presence immediately, but then he smiles and holds the door open for Beth and me.

He's balding, with a plain face, but he has very soft brown eyes and a kind smile. I smile back at him, thanking him.

"Of course. Sorry I almost ran you down. Welcome to Eagle's Rest."

I wonder who he is. Maybe a relative of a resident or a staff member. He looks very nice, and he makes me feel better about being here.

When we get into the lobby, we're greeted by a staff member named Charlotte. She looks to be around forty with just a little extra padding on her—maybe size 14 or 16, about my size—and brown hair pulled back in a ponytail. She has the kind of washed-out face that makes her look like she's been at the back of the closet for too long.

She has a very nice smile, though, and it seems sincere as she welcomes us and shows us back to my new place.

"You've got one of my favorite apartments," she says, turning her head to look back at me. I can tell she's used to walking quickly, getting things done efficiently, and she has to consciously slow herself down to my pace with the walker. "It's on the corner on the ground floor, and it has a lovely view of the gardens. It's east facing, so you can see the sunrise if you wake up early enough."

"I'm always up before dawn." I haven't been able to sleep in past six o'clock for years. It's just one of those things that happened to me as I got older.

"It will be so nice to be able to make a cup of tea and sit down to watch the sunrise when you wake up," Beth says, still trying to be cheerful. She's carrying my bag with the stuff I needed this morning that couldn't be packed up with the rest of my possessions and brought over by Roger.

"Your nephew is in the apartment now," Charlotte tells me, turning right at the end of the hall and waiting for me to catch up. "He's been working hard to get it set up for you."

It's very nice of Roger to help me out this way. He's always been a good nephew, particularly after his mother died. I'm glad to have him. And I'm glad to have Beth. I don't have much family, but I certainly can't complain about the family I have.

There are photographs lining the wall of this hallway, and I glance at them as I walk. They are clearly of residents of Eagle's Rest performing different activities on the grounds. I'm sure they're hung there to give the impression of the community being a fun and social place to live.

I'm not particularly impressed, though. I've never liked tennis, and I've never liked bridge. There's one picture of residents dancing, and I shudder at the idea of going to a dance.

There's one nice photo of people drinking tea in the garden, and that's the only activity that looks like something I would enjoy.

I pause at that picture, caught at first by the lovely colors of the garden and then by the teacups on the table.

But then I notice something else. *Someone* else. My breath hitches slightly as I recognize a man standing in the background.

He has gray, thinning hair and a body that is really not bad for his age—with shoulders that are still broad and straight and only a slight paunch around his middle. But what captures my attention are his features—the broad forehead, the strong nose, the chin with the cleft.

"Is this Dave Andrews?" I ask, peering at the photo and wondering if I've mistaken him somehow.

"Yes," Charlotte says, walking back and looking at the picture with me. "Yes, that's Dave. Do you know him?"

"I used to. He worked at my college for five years. I didn't realize he was still in the area."

"He moved in with us about seven years ago. He had one of the cottages for a long time, but last year he moved into this building. He's very popular with the female residents. If you know him, that won't be a surprise." She gives me a little smile, as if we share a secret.

I return the smile, deciding I like Charlotte. She isn't really as back-of-the-closet as she seemed at first. She's clever and has a sense of humor, and she would be a lot prettier if she'd wear her hair down. Her claim about Dave Andrews doesn't surprise me at all. He was married when I knew him before, but all the girls had been crazy about him anyway. He was one of those guys who could charm anyone—good-looking and used to getting his way because of it.

I hadn't liked him at all. I didn't—and still don't—like those charming, schmoozing kind of men. I don't trust the kind of appeal that comes too easily.

Plus, I had other reasons not to like Dave. He was brought in to get finances under control at the college, which meant he was going around cutting lines in everyone's budgets. He'd thought the library was a money pit, and he hadn't been afraid to tell me so.

I hadn't appreciated it, and I hadn't been afraid to tell him so.

Five years I spent fighting battles with him as he tried to gut the integrity of the college library. He finally got tired of dealing with academics and returned to corporate finance. I'd heard he moved to D.C., and I wonder now if he came back just for the retirement community or if he'd come back before he moved to Eagle's Rest.

He hadn't seemed to really like this area before, being more of a big-city guy, but maybe that has changed.

Shrugging off the memories, I turn away from the photo and keep walking. At the end of the hall is my new apartment.

It's a studio apartment with a private alcove for the bed. It's four hundred square feet with high ceilings and some good sunlight that comes in from the windows on two walls and a French door that leads out onto a small patio.

There's a door that opens to an updated bathroom, and there's a small kitchenette on one wall with a sink, half-size refrigerator, microwave, and electric kettle. Roger has been busy putting up my books on the bookcases he brought in for me, positioning a new recliner near the window, and laying out my pictures and wall hangings where he thought they might go.

It's a decent room. It doesn't feel too much like a hospital, although the bed, sofa, and small table and chairs that come with the room are quite generic.

It isn't home, but it will be okay. I can live here.

I'll have to live here.

"What do you think?" Roger asks with a broad smile.

"It's nice." I walk over to look out the window. Not only does it have a view of the garden, but it also has a view of the woods beyond. "It's very nice."

"I love all the sunshine," Charlotte says, walking over to open the blinds a bit more.

"Yes, that's very nice." I smile at Roger. "Thank you so much for getting it ready."

"Of course. Just tell me where you want the pictures on the wall, and I'll hang them for you."

He knows I never feel at home in a place until the pictures are hung.

We're busy for an hour or two, and then Roger and Beth finally hug me and say good-bye. I'm left alone in the room.

It's really quite pleasant. It could be so much worse. I'm not going to feel sorry for myself or complain when I've ended up in a very nice home.

I find my comb in my bag and carry it to the bathroom, where I put it down on the vanity.

As I do, I catch a glimpse of myself in the mirror, and I look so old I barely recognize myself.

Maybe it's just the lighting here. It's different from my bathroom in the house. Since I've always carried a little extra weight, my face isn't as wrinkled as a lot of women's my age, but I see the creases on my forehead and at the corners of my mouth and eyes that stand out in stark detail at the moment.

My eyes are blue, and my hair is steel gray, hanging down to my shoulders since I always had long hair and still can't bring myself to cut it all off.

I used to wear red lipstick, and I think about putting it on now to brighten up my face before I go down for dinner.

I don't, though.

My lipstick days are over—just like my days of having a dog are over. I'm not going to be one of those silly women who can't let go of her younger self and so becomes slightly ridiculous.

I've always been intelligent, independent, and practical. That's what I'll continue to be.

I can be so here too.

I'm surprised when there's a tap on the door to my apartment, and I turn too quickly and jar my hip painfully.

So I'm slower than usual as I shuffle to the door to open it.

It's Charlotte, smiling at me. "I'm just checking to make sure everything's all right."

"Yes, it's very nice. Thank you."

"I'll go down with you to dinner, if you want. I know it's not always easy going alone if you're new to a place. Some folks have told me it's like the first day of school."

It's a very kind thought, and I accept it. I grab my crocheted handbag and start down with her.

"How long have you worked here?" I ask as we go.

"Almost twelve years now."

"You enjoy it?"

"I do. I really do."

"Do you have children?" I ask because I'm curious —no other reason than that.

She shakes her head. "I always wanted them, but it's not looking like it's going to happen."

"Well, you never know. I doubt it's too late for you yet."

She gives a little laugh. "It's getting there."

"So you're not married?"

"No."

"Do you have a boyfriend?"

"I . . . I think so."

That answer doesn't seem promising—nor does the slight twisting of her face as she says it. If a woman isn't able to say confidently that she has a boyfriend, then it's likely she doesn't.

But I like Charlotte and I don't want to hurt her feelings, so I just nod. "That's good."

"His name is Kevin. He's a lawyer. Oh, actually, Dave Andrews is his stepfather."

"Oh, really?" I try to sound interested, since I know she just mentions it because I brought up Dave to her before.

"He's out of town. Dave, I mean. Well, actually, both Dave and Kevin. The family took a trip to Niagara Falls. They won't be back until next week."

The truth is I don't care all that much about Dave.

It's of no interest to me whether he's in town or not. I didn't like him before, so I'm not inclined to like him now.

I do like Charlotte, and something tells me that Kevin, the lawyer, isn't the kind of boyfriend she deserves.

three

I used to always get butterflies on the first day of school. I'd be excited about my new classes, my new teacher, my new classmates. I'd imagine all the wonderful, exciting things that would happen to me that year.

Despite what Charlotte said, the butterflies were entirely lacking when I went down to the dining room last night. Charlotte found me a seat at a table with a kind couple and a rather absentminded woman in her eighties who asked me three times if I liked to knit. They were all perfectly nice, but it's hardly what I'd call exciting.

Marjorie, the knitting inquirer, invited me to hang out in the TV room after dinner. It appears that's a popular evening destination, since I saw several people heading in that direction.

Instead, I went up to my room and watched an old British mystery on my own television.

I went to bed early.

This morning, I wake up early, as I always do. Breakfast doesn't start being served until seven, so I make myself a cup of tea, take it out to my patio, and do a crossword as I wait for the sun to rise. It's very quiet, with just a few early birds chirping in the trees and the sound of the trash truck coming at one point to empty the facility's dumpster.

I'm used to quiet mornings, so I'm perfectly happy until it's light enough outside for me to want to take a walk up to the woods to see my dogs.

That's impossible, of course.

There's no reason I can't take a walk, though. I can see the path that follows the perimeter of the woods toward the valley overlook. It's still more than an hour before breakfast begins. I have plenty of time.

I could call to ask for assistance in dressing, but I'm not inclined to do that unless I have to. I'm still perfectly capable of taking care of myself. It's just the household chores that were getting hard for me. I take showers in the evening before bed, so it's no problem for me now to put on my clothes, wash my face, and brush my hair.

I used to always wear flowing tops or dresses and striking beads around my neck, which I collected wherever I could find them. I still have my bead collection, but it feels like a lot of effort to wear them anymore. After all, the highlight of my days now will probably be going to the dining room to eat. So I stick with a casual pair of pants and a simple top, making sure I have the call button that all residents are given in case of emergency. I'm yearning for a dog as I make my way to the back door of the building and walk outside.

The back gardens lead to the walking paths, and I

follow the one I want. It's slow going because my hip is still weak and my knees and ankles feel sore from my normal arthritis. But I can support myself on my walker, and it's really not a very long walk until I reach a bench that offers a good view of the valley.

I lower myself onto the bench, pulling my walker up next to me so it's not blocking the view but is still in easy reach.

I look. And I breathe.

It's the same Valentine Valley that I've known and loved for so long, with the gentle, tree-lined slopes falling down into the bowl, the lake just east of the center, and the familiar pattern of roads breaking through the woods. This is the opposite side, however, so I'm not looking across at the top of the heart.

It looks different. Vaguely unfamiliar. It's unsettling.

I tell myself not to be stupid about it. A view from the wrong direction is better than no view at all. I entertain myself by trying to make out buildings I know on the far side, although it's such a distance that it's mostly just a guessing game.

I stay on the bench for a long time, and I feel better when I finally get up and make my way back to the building for breakfast.

I can do this.

This situation is not perfect—not shaped as exactly right for me as the three-branch seat on the old oak tree was. It's more like that one branch higher up: not exactly comfortable, but stable enough to hold me and keep me from tumbling all the way down.

I have tea that afternoon with the spacey knitting lady named Marjorie. Not that she actually knits. I haven't seen her do so, at least. But she seems fond of asking me whether I do, so I assume it's something she's enjoyed at some point in her life.

Marjorie's skin is like crumpled white paper, and her arms are so thin and frail I'm quite sure I could break one of her bones without even exerting myself.

That's a macabre thought. Just so it's clear, I would never actually do such a thing.

Earlier, when I carried my tea out to the veranda, Marjorie smiled, so I went over to sit at the table with her. It's a sunny afternoon, and many of the residents have had the same idea. Most of the tables are full. Some of the men and women look at me, and I can't help but wonder what they're thinking.

I focus on Marjorie, since I've met her and she's right in front of me.

"Are you enjoying your day?" she asks, stirring her tea with a little spoon.

"It's been very nice. Thank you. I'm still getting used to everything, of course."

"It's lovely here. I'm sure you'll find it lovely. Do you like to knit?"

I shake my head soberly. "I've never learned to knit or crochet or do any sort of handiwork."

Her eyes widen, as if this admission is astonishing. "Oh, dear. I'm sorry to hear it."

"I've managed all right so far without it." I make sure my tone is gentle, since I don't want to sound sarcastic.

"We have a knitting circle that meets every Wednesday afternoon, but if you don't knit, you'd be bored there, I'm afraid."

"Probably so. I'll have to miss out. Thank you for the thought, though." This is the first time she's mentioned the knitting circle, and I'm pleased to know there is actually a purpose to her questioning.

"What do you like to do then?"

"I enjoy crosswords and other word games. I read too."

"Oh, you do?"

"I was a librarian for a long time."

"A librarian! How lovely. My eyes are so bad now I can't do any reading."

I wonder how her failing vision might affect her knitting, but I don't ask about it. "I also like to take walks, at least as much as I can with this new hip."

"Walking is so good for your health."

I smile. "It is."

"We have walking paths here you should try."

"I've already done so. I took a walk this morning to the bench that looks out on Valentine Valley. It was lovely."

"Oh." Marjorie's brown eyes go wider than normal. "Oh. Oh. The bench?"

"Yes," I reply slowly, startled by her dramatic reaction. "Do you know the one I mean?"

"Yes. Oh, yes. That's Dave's bench."

I frown. "What do you mean it's his bench?"

"It's *his* bench." She looks very concerned for a few moments, clucking her tongue and stirring her tea vigorously. Then she relaxes and lets out a breath. "Oh, it's all right then. He's out of town this week, isn't he?"

I can only assume she means Dave Andrews, since Charlotte also told me he's out of town this week, going to visit Niagara Falls with his family. My spine stiffens with annoyance at the idea that he would claim a bench that is clearly part of the common grounds and property and thus available for any of the residents.

Maybe it's just one of Marjorie's eccentricities. I can hardly assume Dave has been selfish and entitled with no more evidence than one old lady claiming the bench is his.

"I don't know," I say, careful not to convey any feeling. "But I assume I'm allowed to sit on the bench if I take a walk in the mornings."

"He's not here this week," Marjorie says, smiling at me in her genial way again. "So it's not a problem."

This annoys me, but I don't want to be one of those crabby, irritable old women I used to laugh at. I push the thought out of my mind.

After all, I am going to walk to the bench every morning and look out to the valley. So there is no reason to be annoyed by the thought of anyone trying to stop me.

The week goes quickly, although each individual day seems to drag. I'm not sure how that happens, but it sometimes does. At three o'clock in the afternoon, it feels like it's been an eternity since morning, but when I wake up in the morning it feels like a new day can't possibly be here already.

Whatever the reason, it's Saturday before I know it. The weekends don't feel any different to me than weekdays do now, but I still always wake up on Saturdays with a happy feeling and the idea that I'm allowed to take it easy today.

When I was living in the house, what that meant was not doing any of the daily chores and fixing something easy for meals. Here, it doesn't mean much of anything at all, since I neither cook nor clean.

I lie in bed for a few minutes, trying to decide if

there's anything slightly different I can do to mark the day as a Saturday. There's a bus to a shopping mall this afternoon that I can join, but I've never enjoyed shopping—particularly from large chain stores—so that seems like a lot of effort for no enjoyment.

I can skip my walk, since that's my main exertion for the day, but it's also the thing I enjoy the most, so I'm not about to miss out on it.

I can call Roger and Beth to see how they're doing. Roger has called a couple of times this week to check in, but Saturday is a good day for a longer chat.

That will be something. Then maybe I can choose one activity to participate in today instead of spending all my free time in my apartment, as I've been doing.

I'm pleased with this plan, and I'm in a good mood as I go outside just after the sun rises and take my normal path. The walk has gotten a little easier, even with just the days that have passed this week. That's encouraging.

Perhaps soon I can graduate to a cane rather than using the awkward walker.

I've started taking a book with me in the mornings, so I'll have something to do should I decide to stay a little longer. The path is as quiet as ever, and the bench is inviting and solitary as I approach. It's backed by two lovely weeping willows, and one of the branches is low enough for the lacy leaves to brush the back edge of the bench.

I take my place, moving my walker out of the way and breathing deeply of the cool air. It's the first day of September, and at the moment it's starting to feel like fall. It even smells like fall—that damp, earthy smell that gets wafted with the cool breeze.

I love when summer ends. I always have. I find the heat and humidity oppressive. Years of working in a school setting has ingrained September as the time of new starts, fresh opportunity, brand new school years waiting to be filled with anything.

For the first time in a long time—in at least two months—I feel a kind of pulsing in my blood. Not excitement, really, but genuine enjoyment.

There's fog out in the valley this morning, covering the trees with thick, wet grayness, some of the edges of the clouds breaking out in silver when hit by a stream of sunlight.

It's like the valley is asleep, just on the edge of awakening.

"What are you doing here?"

The voice is startling, unexpected, rough with what sounds like displeasure. I give a little jump in response and turn to see a man standing a ways down the path. He's clearly come up from the main buildings as I have.

It's Dave Andrews. He's changed with the years,

just as everyone does, but he's still unmistakable with his straight posture and cleft chin. He has stopped walking and is glowering at me.

I have no idea what his problem is, so I say the obvious thing. "Excuse me?"

"What are you doing on the bench?"

I remember Marjorie's worried tone as she said the bench was Dave's. For a moment, I feel a familiar shiver of concern at having broken a rule. I've never been particularly rebellious, and I've always hated getting in trouble.

Then I come to my senses. I haven't broken any rule. This bench is part of Eagle's Rest and is not Dave's personal property. I have nothing to be ashamed of here.

I lift my eyebrows, determined not to let him put me at a disadvantage. He always used to, when we worked together. "I'm sitting. Is there a problem?"

He comes closer, still glaring. He walks a lot better than I do. He must not have a bad hip or knee. He's a few years older than me, I believe, but he seems to be in pretty good shape.

His attitude . . . well, that's something entirely different.

"It's my bench."

Now I'm getting really annoyed. "Your bench?"

"Yes, my bench."

"I don't see your name on it."

There is a sudden little gleam in his dark eyes, a

look I remember from when he believed he'd scored a victory in one of our old debates about the budget. "Look on the back."

With a very slight eye roll, I lean back slightly and look down. There, to my great exasperation, I see words engraved on the stone. *In memory of Clara Andrews.*

His wife, maybe. I can't remember her name, and I never met her, since Dave and I only interacted at work.

"I assume that's to acknowledge who donated money for the bench. If that was you, then I'm sure it was a very generous gesture. But that doesn't mean no one else is allowed to sit on the bench. I understood it belonged to Eagle's Rest."

He's still frowning, clearly displeased by my stubbornness and cool tone. "I always sit here in the mornings."

I clear my throat and nod toward the empty half of the bench. "There is plenty of room. Please feel free to sit down if you'd like."

He stands for another minute, looming over me. I assume he's trying to intimidate me or pressure me into leaving. A lot of people probably would cave, not wanting to cause conflict or not caring enough to hold out against resistance.

I do care, though. I've been walking here every morning, and I intend to continue just as long as I can.

Plus, his attitude is obnoxious. He might be grayer now, his body less lean and hard than it used to be, but he's still the same Dave Andrews. Acting as though the world belongs to him, like he knows better than anyone, assuming people will dash out of his way simply because he's coming through.

He doesn't even remember me. I clearly made no lasting impression on him back then.

That's annoying too.

I've felt this way over and over again in my life—a kind of disappointment when I realize that I haven't had the impact on someone that I wanted. I remember being crushed in school when I wasn't invited to a certain party, one thrown by a girl I believed was my friend. Or there were library symposiums and workshops organized and implemented, and no one thought to invite me, even though I had more experience and knowledge of certain fields than the speakers who were invited.

There's always been a kind of invisibility to me, and I've never understood why.

It's not something that has troubled me in the last couple of decades, but I feel that old disappointment again, sitting here on the bench, with a breeze bringing with it a taste of the fall, like it did when I was a girl and heading for my first day of school.

I remember Dave—quite well, in fact, although he certainly hasn't been someone I thought much about in the intervening years. I'd like to think he would remember me too.

He obviously doesn't. There's no hint of recognition on his face. Just general bad temper, as if I'm some pesky stranger he doesn't want to see.

So I don't get up, and I don't scoot over to give him more room, although I could if I wanted to be polite. I stay exactly as I'm situated when he sits down beside me, stretching his legs out and releasing a throaty huff.

Old men are often spoiled, sulking when they don't get their way. Dave was the kind of arrogant, entitled man who is probably more spoiled now than others.

My enjoyment of the morning is entirely gone, but I'm not going to cave. I keep a calm expression as I gaze out on the valley for a few minutes and then pick up my book and pretend to read.

I'm not reading. I can't possibly concentrate—not with Dave Andrews sitting next to me, bristling with displeasure. But I'd like him to think he doesn't faze me at all.

I can sense him looking over at me occasionally. I have no idea what he's thinking. I wonder if he likes to come out here to look at the view, like I do, or if he just walks for exercise and only stopped because he saw someone on the bench he claims as his.

After about twenty minutes, my hip is getting stiff,

and it's past time for me to go back to the residence. It's nearly seven. Time for breakfast.

But I don't want to leave before Dave does. That would feel like a defeat.

The whole time, he's been sitting stiffly, staring out at the valley for the most part. So I'm surprised when he asks gruffly, "So you're here now, are you?"

I turn toward him and realize that he's recognized me after all. Maybe he recognized me from the beginning, or maybe my identity finally clicked in his mind. "Yes, I'm here."

He makes a sound that's something like "hmph" and stands up.

He mutters before he walks away, "You go away for a week and everything changes."

I have no idea what he means by that, unless he thinks some random woman sitting on a bench is a disruption to his entire life.

Surely he's not so melodramatic. Or maybe he is. I really can't remember.

And I don't care.

I watch him walk away, feeling irrationally victorious, like I've accomplished something worthwhile, something that really needed to be done.

It's not a bad day's work, after all—taking Dave Andrews down a peg or two. And it isn't even seven o'clock in the morning.

four

When I first went to college, I was determined to start over, to become what I called a "Brand New Ellie." No more shy, retiring bookworm. I was going to be social, friendly, the life of the party like my sister always was. Girls would want to hang out with me, and boys would want to date me.

I was just seventeen my freshman year and still living at home. Back then, this wasn't unusual, and the private liberal arts college near my home had organized a number of socials the first few weeks to give new students opportunities to get acclimated and get to know each other.

I tried. I stretched myself so much in those weeks that I fell into bed exhausted at the end of every day. I introduced myself to strangers. I chatted with classmates instead of finding a quiet corner to read. I acted like I was confident, outgoing, a social butterfly.

I'm not sure it ever really worked. I met people, but by the end of the first semester, I was back to where I'd always been—hanging out alone a lot, with just a few good friends.

I still remember the sort of pressure I felt back then, this need to be someone different in order to properly engage a new situation. And I feel it again as I get dressed on Saturday evening for a dance.

A *dance*. To be specific, a "Big Band Dance Shindig." Yes, that's actually what they're calling it.

I know I told myself I wasn't going to bother with silly activities like this, but I've been here less than a week and I've met about five people total. Marjorie says I should go to the dance. Charlotte says I should go to the dance. And I feel this ridiculous urge to prove myself to the rest of the residents—particularly Dave Andrews.

I should be well past this sort of implicit peer pressure, but it turns out I'm not. Maybe you never really are, when you're put in the right (or wrong) situation. Anyway, here I am, putting on a dark blue flowing skirt and one of my favorite printed tops—one that makes me look curvy rather than plump. I look in the mirror as I comb out my hair, pulling back just the top half with a clip.

I figure I look nice enough, but then I put on my old red lipstick. "Ellie Red," the students used to call it at the college. Maybe they were having a little fun at my expense—the quirky librarian who was a fixture at the school and always wore the same red lipstick—but it seemed good-natured, so I never minded.

It's nice to be known for something, even if it's just the shade of your lipstick.

I hesitate, wondering if I'm dressed enough for

the evening. I know some of the women here will be dressed to the nines, using any opportunity available to pull out their expensive jewelry and sparkling apparel. But that's not me. It's never been me. I open the small chest where I keep all my necklaces and pull out a string of silver beads.

They fall down to just between my breasts, and they pull my outfit together nicely.

There. I've made an effort. In all likelihood, I'll sit in a chair and pretend to be having fun for an hour before I can finally make an escape. But I told Marjorie I'd go down with her, and I have too strong a conscience to disappoint her over a silly case of cold feet.

I pick up my bag, smooth down my skirt, and make sure all of my clothes are in the right place before I walk down the hall to Marjorie's room. She's giggling as she opens the door, dressed in a pink silk dress that looks like it must have been bought in the seventies. I think she looks pretty and carefree, though, and I'm vaguely jealous of her ability to have fun and not overthink these kinds of occasions.

I knew a lot of girls like her in school. They always quickly had boyfriends and never took life too seriously. In other words, they were polar opposites of people like me.

"You look beautiful," she says, eyeing me from top to bottom. "I'm so jealous of your lovely skin."

When I was younger, people used to say that my

skin was my best feature, clear and firm and rosy, but it's definitely not what it once was.

I thank her for the compliment and give her a few of my own, and then we head down the hall and outside, walking next door to the community building.

I can hear the music even before we get inside, paired with the chattering of voices. It's a big night, evidently. It looks like nearly everyone in the residence is here.

A tottering bald gentleman in a seersucker suit asks Marjorie to dance right away. She goes off with him, smiling and clearly ready to enjoy herself.

It's such a familiar scene that I almost laugh—albeit ironically. Over seventy and still left on my own at a dance, feeling like an idiot.

There are plenty of people in chairs around the edges of the room, talking and watching the dancing. Not everyone is healthy enough to dance, and fortunately I have the excuse of the walker, making it obvious that I'm not dance material at the moment.

I'll just find a seat and start up a conversation with someone nearby. If it's too boring, I'll leave after a while.

I'm far too old to feel awkward or self-conscious in a situation like this.

My pep talk helps to a certain extent, and I'm scanning the room for an empty chair when Charlotte appears beside me.

"There's a seat over here," she says with a smile,

gently turning me toward the left. "I'm so glad you made it. Everyone is having a fantastic time."

I wonder if that's actually true. Certainly, most of the people in the room are smiling, talking, laughing, or dancing, but there's a thing that goes on at social gatherings like this. Sometimes it feels to me like we're all just desperately talking ourselves into having fun, convincing ourselves it's real. I wonder how many men and women here are in pain or bored or incredibly lonely—even as they put on a cheerful facade.

This is what I mean about overthinking occasions like this. I've done it all my life. I can hardly be surprised that I never seem to enjoy them.

I follow Charlotte to the side of the room, and I'm grateful for the seat she offers me. It's a leather-padded metal chair, and it's straight and sturdy enough for me to sit in comfortably.

She introduces me to the woman on my right—Nancy with a steel-gray bun and a perpetually crabby expression. Then she goes off to get me a cup of tea, since I prefer that to the punch most of the others are drinking.

I say a few words to Nancy, but she's clearly less of a conversationalist than I am.

I'm startled when a white-haired man with a thick mustache comes over, looks down at me, and quite seriously says, "Lovely. Lovely. Would you do me the honor of becoming my wife?"

I lift my eyebrows and reply with equal serious-ness, "I really don't think so, but thank you for the offer."

He looks not the least bit perturbed as he wanders away with a slight limp on his left leg, muttering, "Lovely. Lovely."

I turn to look at Nancy.

She shakes her head. "The fool is always propos-ing to someone."

Well, that's an ego boost, isn't it? I'm just one in a long line of propose-ees. The episode tickles me, and I'm having a private laugh when Charlotte returns with my tea.

"Did I see Mr. Draycott proposing to you?"

"Oh, yes. I was starting to plan out the wedding when he just wandered off."

Charlotte smiles, obviously understanding and appreciating my humor. "Isn't that always the way with men? Start to plan out the wedding and then they're just . . ." She trails off, as if a less happy thought has occurred to her.

I'm sure it has to do with Kevin, the lawyer, her would-be boyfriend. Interested in hearing more, I ask lightly, "So no wedding bells in your future?"

Charlotte looks down at her hands. "Oh. I don't know. I don't think so."

For a moment, I feel intensely sympathetic. I've been in that situation myself a few times—ages ago now.

"Well," I murmur, "if the man you've got isn't giving you what you need, maybe it's time to move on to someone else."

She shakes her head. "That's good advice, but not so easy. They're not exactly beating down my door, you know."

Of course I did.

"They weren't for me either," I reply with a smile. "And look at me now, the life of the party."

She understands the light irony and smiles in response. Then her expression changes. "I don't know. I've noticed quite a few gentlemen here who seem to have taken an interest in you."

She's being kind. Obviously. No one is paying any sort of attention to me. But my eyes immediately shoot over to Dave Andrews, who is dancing with an overly made-up redhead in a sequined dress far too tight for her figure.

Yes, I noticed Dave immediately, as soon as I walked into the room, but I'm trying not to give him any more of my attention than he deserves.

He looks quite distinguished in a gray suit and very shiny shoes. It's not hard to recognize, simply from watching the reactions of people around him, that he's the rooster of this particular chicken house.

I don't like him, and I don't like the fact that he's made any sort of impression on me. In the few seconds my eyes are on him, he looks in my direction and meets my gaze.

I have no idea what he's thinking, and I look away almost immediately. I've made a point all my life of never being a silly woman. I'm not going to start now.

I turn back to Charlotte, who is nodding across the room. "Gordon Marcus, for instance, can't keep his eyes off you."

The name rings a bell. And then I recognize the face of the man who is seated in a chair directly across from me with a glass of punch in his hands.

Gordon Marcus. It must be the same man. I went out with him for a couple of months in my twenties. A solid, white-bread, polite young man who was working his way through medical school.

We got along fairly well, and I certainly would have continued dating him, but he stopped asking me out and that was that.

Most of my relationships ended that way. No huge blowup or dramatic angst—just a slow fizzling out.

Gordon obviously recognizes me, though, since he nods and smiles when our eyes meet. I give him an answering smile and a little wave, and I'm pleased when he stands up and starts to make his way over to me.

"You know him?" Charlotte asks.

"Yes, he's an old boyfriend of mine. Nothing serious, but we went out a long time ago."

"Well, it's the perfect time for firing up old acquaintances." Charlotte gives me a little wink and leaves just as Gordon comes over.

He takes the chair she vacated and says, "It's Ellie Davenport, isn't it?"

"It is. Good memory. I had no idea you were here too."

"I've been here for just over two years. I saw you earlier in the week and have been waiting to say hello."

My eyes widen. "Why didn't you say hello earlier?"

He gives a little shrug. He looks just as solid and white-bread as he did as a young man. He's pleasant enough to look at, and I like the friendliness in his brown eyes. "I thought about it, but there wasn't a good opportunity." He pauses, then adds sheepishly, "To tell you the truth, you looked like you didn't want company, and I didn't want to bother you."

So that's not exactly what I want to hear. Evidently, I've been giving off a keep-away vibe, even to an old friend like Gordon.

It's not that I never want to talk to people. It's that this is entirely new and I'm not comfortable yet, and I've always been more secure when I keep my own company.

"I guess I'm just trying to get used to it here," I say, hoping a friendly smile will counter that standoffishness I've been exuding. "I'm very glad to see you here. So you stayed in the area after medical school?"

"Yes. I was a surgeon in Roanoke for over forty years. I came here after my wife died." He looks around the room, nodding with what looks like satisfaction. "It's a nice place. I'm glad you joined us."

"Thank you."

"So did you ever get married?"

I hate that question—not because it bothers me that I've been unmarried all my life but because so many people seem to think it's a sign of failure that I never managed to snag a husband. But there's no sense in lying about it, unless I'm prepared to concoct an elaborate backstory and manufacture evidence in support of it.

"Oh, no. I never did. I went to graduate school and became a university librarian."

"Oh, excellent. A career woman. I should have known you had it in you." He grins at me affably, and—as far as I can tell—his admiration is genuine.

"I had a very nice career," I say. "And a good life. I hope the same is true of you."

"Very good. Very good. Four children, you know."

"Oh, excellent. And what are they all doing now?"

He tells me about his children and grandchildren for a while, and I'm surprised by how quickly the time passes.

As Gordon and I talk, Dave has four different dance partners.

Yes, I've counted them. It's not like I set out to do so. I just notice every time a song ends and he goes around to find someone else to dance with.

He doesn't even really ask the women. He just sticks out his hand and assumes the woman will stand up and walk out to the dance floor with him. He's not a flashy dancer like a couple of the others in the room, but he's certainly competent. And not a single woman turns him down.

I don't know why it annoys me as much as it does. It's that smug entitlement, I think—that assumption he can have anything he wants.

The bench.

Any of the women in the room.

Anything he wants.

I would have thought that, living as long as he has, some of that arrogance would have been burned off through the fires of life, but evidently it hasn't been.

He's still the same jackass who showed up in my office one day and told me my budget for periodicals would be cut in half starting immediately.

Needless to say, my response to this outrageous claim was neither gentle nor polite.

"Do you know Dave then?" Gordon asks, noticing my preoccupation.

I curse myself for being rude and turn my attention back to my companion. "He worked at my college for a few years. He was the money guy."

"Was he? I guess he wasn't very popular then."

"No. Not really."

"That must be why you were frowning at him."

I hadn't realized I was frowning before, although it's not surprising given the turn of my thoughts.

"That was a long time ago," I say, shaping my expression to be light and pleasant. "I'm sure he's a very nice man."

Gordon shakes his head. "I don't know about that."

"He's not a nice man?" I'm interested—for obvious reasons.

"I guess he's okay. Just doesn't make much of an effort. You know?"

I know exactly, no matter how vague his words are. It's precisely my problem with Dave too. People who are able to take what they want without working too hard at it just rub me the wrong way. I like Gordon even better for recognizing it and for responding to the quality the same way I do.

We like to have our impressions validated by other people. And the less generous they are, the more we like to have them validated.

"He looks popular," I murmur, as Dave finishes his dance with a plump bleached blonde with ridiculously high heels and eyes the room, obviously looking for his next partner.

His eyes land on me for a moment, and I quickly look away.

He's not likely to ask me to dance, given our conversation that morning. But, if he does, I'm certainly going to say no.

"All the ladies like him," Gordon says, shaking his head as if this is a source of ire for him. "As you can see."

"I guess there's a lot of competition here," I begin, looking around and easily picking up undertones in looks and postures and interactions. "For partners, I mean. There are so many more women than men."

"I suppose so. Everyone wants to be coupled up."

I give Gordon a curious look. "You haven't found someone then?"

A brief flicker of grief crosses his face. "I had someone for nearly a year. She passed away just over a month ago."

"Oh, I'm very sorry. What was her name?"

"Wendy. She was wonderful." He sighs. "But, onward, right?"

"Right."

It strikes me as a sad thing to say. *Onward.* After you've lost someone you love. There's not much else for one to do, however, since life goes on whether we want it to or not.

I notice Marjorie standing in a corner of the room, and I wave at her cheerfully.

She waves back, smiling endlessly, but I notice that she's fidgety, as if she's bored or restless or discontent. She's only danced once, as far as I can tell. It would be nice if someone would dance with her again. She's obviously waiting for it, since she hasn't found a seat like many of the others.

As I watch, Dave walks over and offers his hand to Marjorie. She's clearly thrilled, and she giggles as she goes out to the dance floor with him.

She's probably several years older than him, and she's not as attractive as the other women he's been dancing with, so it feels like a gesture of kindness to me.

One I never would have expected from him.

"That's nice," Gordon murmurs, obviously recognizing it too. "Everyone loves Marjorie. I'm glad she's getting to dance."

"You should get out there," I say, pushing aside the silly little flutter of appreciation. This isn't an Austen novel, after all. One little gesture that costs Dave nothing isn't any sort of sign of his nobility or a good heart hiding under his spoiled nature.

As far as I can tell, he doesn't have a good heart at all.

"I have a bum knee," Gordon says, "but I can give it a try if you want to join me."

I shake my head, pleased with the words, as if I'm important enough to affect his choices.

You don't grow out of that. You don't get too old for it to mean something to you.

"I don't think I'm up to it quite yet, after my hip surgery. And I've never been much of a dancer."

"I'll just keep you company here then."

He does keep me company—for a good hour until the dancers were wearing out and some of the residents have started leaving.

I'm getting tired myself, as pleasant as Gordon's

conversation is. Social situations always drain me, and I need to get back on my own to recover.

So I say good night to Gordon, smile and wave at a few acquaintances, including Marjorie, and start to the door of the room.

As I'm leaving, Dave Andrews is coming back in. I don't know where he went, although I was aware of his disappearing about five minutes ago.

He may have just gone to use the restroom.

I almost bump into him, and I have to stabilize myself on my walker.

"Oh," I say, startled and off balance. "Try to watch where you're going."

"The same could be said of you."

I roll my eyes. "That's not very gallant."

"You're expecting gallantry?"

"No." I give him a cool glare, since his tone was dry and lofty, exactly the kind of tone that annoys me the most. "I don't expect anything of the kind."

"I see you've made a friend," Dave says, glancing into the room, where Gordon is having a chat with a few other residents.

It's none of his business whether I've made a friend or not, so I decide not to answer.

"Just be careful. He was in a relationship with a woman who died recently, so he's not yet emotionally available."

Maybe his advice is given out in a genuine attempt

to help, but I don't really think so. He sounds snide, as if he's pleased that the man who has showed interest in me can't really want me for real.

"Well, you'd know all about emotional unavailability, wouldn't you?"

As soon as I say it, I wish I hadn't. It's been a long time since I believed that kind of empty banter is constructive or worthwhile.

He doesn't even react except to almost smile, as if something amuses him. "Maybe. So how are you enjoying Eagle's Rest after your first week?"

It's the first mostly civil thing he's said to me since we met this morning. "I don't really know," I say, speaking the truth. "It's kind of like being in school again, isn't it?"

He gives a dry chuckle. "Yes. And the longer you're here, the more it feels that way."

I don't know exactly how to respond to that—I'm not sure whether it's encouraging to know that other people feel the way I do or depressing to know it's never going to change. I end up nodding my farewell and continuing down the hall.

I feel like he might be watching me as I leave him, but I don't turn my head to look back.

five

*T*he next morning, I wake up a little later than usual, so I don't have as long to drink tea and sit on my patio, watching the sun slowly rise behind the mountains.

There are rarely true sunrises around here. Usually, the sky just gradually lightens, since the sun itself is hidden behind a mountain until it's too far up in the sky for there to be stunning shades of pink and orange on display.

Sometimes, you get lucky if you're in exactly the right position. But, from my patio, all I see is that slow lightening of the sky.

It's Sunday, and it's common practice for people to sleep in today—I assume that's true of the residents of Eagle's Rest as much as it is the rest of the world. I don't sleep in, however. I don't think I'm capable of it anymore.

As it is, getting up just after five, I feel like I'm late, like I'm unsettled and out of sorts. I'm more tired than usual, and I know it's from the socializing last night. I stayed up later than I anticipated, and I exerted far more energy in interacting with others than I have in a very long time. I might not have danced, but it was exertion just the same.

I'd been considering going to church this morning, but I decide against it as I sip my first cup of tea. I've gone to church on and off all my life—some periods more off than on—and it still feels to me like an appropriate thing to do on a Sunday morning.

But not this morning. Today, I'll take my walk and then take it easy for the rest of the day. Roger sent me a new book of crosswords yesterday, so I'll start on one of those. Maybe doze and watch a British mystery this afternoon.

There are some folks my age who get bored without orchestrated activities, but I certainly am not one of them.

I'm looking forward to my day as I dress and leave the building for my walk. I still take the walker, but I'm pleased that this morning I don't have to lean on it very much. I just keep it in front of me to stabilize my balance.

I've been active all my life, and perhaps the worst part of getting old is not being able to make my body do what it used to do all the time.

The morning is so cool it's almost brisk. I'm glad I put on a sweater as I feel the breeze blowing my clothes against my skin. It feels like a real fall day— with even more of that earthy autumn scent in the air than I smelled yesterday.

I love it.

My dogs always used to get energized when the weather turned cooler, after being lazy and lethargic all summer. I remember watching them bound across the grass and into the woods on the first genuinely cool day of the fall, and I feel a bit like them this morning.

Not that I'm inclined to go bounding anywhere at the moment—or ever again, for that matter—but still . . . it's a nice thought. It's a nice feeling.

I make it to the bench a few minutes quicker than I've been managing for the last week, and I'm excited about that too. Despite the normal aches in my joints, I'm feeling good this morning. Maybe I'm recovering from the hip surgery at last.

I sit on the bench and breathe the cool air and think encouraging thoughts for about ten minutes. Then I hear a sound down the path coming from the direction of the residence.

I have a faint suspicion about who it might be, and the suspicion is realized when Dave Andrews comes into view.

I'm tempted to turn away and pretend I don't notice him, but this feels a bit too childish to follow through with. They say that old people sometimes turn childish. I don't want that to be true of me.

So I'm watching calmly as he approaches. Like yesterday, he's wearing a pair of jeans and a golf shirt that looks expensive. Like yesterday, he's frowning as he draws near.

"So you're here again."

I'm not sure whether this is a question or statement. Either way, the answer should be self-evident. I just lift my eyebrows and watch as he takes the seat beside me.

"Are you always going to be here?" he asks rather gruffly, giving me an impatient look.

"Not every hour of the day, obviously. But I walk every morning, and this is the view that I particularly like. So, yes, you can expect to find me here in the mornings at about this time."

He doesn't reply. Just gives me a cool look and stares out into the landscape.

It's still summer enough for the leaves on the trees to be green. They're not turning yellow or brown or red yet, so the valley is cast with a uniform green color, broken only by the slashing lines of the roads, the scattering of buildings, and the glinting of the lake.

"I'm sure there are other walks you can take." I make sure to keep my voice composed, as if the conversation is of no interest to me. "If you'd rather not run into me."

"I always walk here."

"Then we'll likely see each other. Please don't feel obliged to talk to me if you'd rather not. I'm used to my own company."

"I know that."

I'm not sure what he means by that last comment. It could be an insinuation, but the tone isn't particularly snide or bitter.

He's a strange man. Not as easy to read as he was when he was younger.

We both stare out at the valley for a few minutes. Then he asks without transition, "Why did you never get married?"

I blink and turn to look at him. "Why do you assume I never did?" The question is a way of stalling, of course, since I have no idea how to answer him.

"I asked about you. They said you didn't. Did you?"

I wonder who "they" is. Then I wonder why Dave has been asking about me at all. I could be flattered, but I'm not. "No. I never got married."

"Why not?"

I give a little shrug, since asking why I never got married is like asking why I became a librarian or why I love dogs or why I wear my hair long.

It's just who I am and how my life turned out. It's not something that can be explained in a few words.

Dave is studying me now, as if he's trying to figure me out, trying to see something on my face. "A few people said, back at the college, that you were gay."

I shake my head. I'm not surprised, nor am I offended. It's not an unreasonable speculation, given my long-unmarried status.

Women of my generation got married. If they didn't, there was something different about them.

I suppose there's something different about me.

Of course, let's be honest and admit there's something different about everyone.

"I'm not gay," I say calmly, giving Dave a little smile so he'll know the question doesn't concern me.

"I didn't think you were. You were living with a man when we worked together, weren't you?"

"Yes. I was." That was Jeff. He was the only man I lived with.

"He didn't want to marry you?"

Now, I'm a little annoyed. "He wanted to marry me. I didn't want to marry him."

"Why not? Holding out for Prince Charming?"

"If that were the case, I would be sadly out of luck, wouldn't I?"

Dave gives a little laugh, the crease in his chin more pronounced than usual. "I guess so."

He seems to accept my refusal to open up on private matters with him, because he doesn't press me any further about my unmarried condition.

After a few minutes, I pick up my book and start to read, and he stares off into the distance without speaking.

I wonder what he's thinking about, but I'm not about to ask him.

I do like that he's able to amuse himself with his own thoughts. It's not something that is true about everyone.

The next day, Dave is sitting on the bench when I approach.

I'm expecting him to show up, since he has the last two days, but seeing him there before me rattles me a bit.

Naturally, I don't show it. I just murmur good morning as I sit down on the bench beside him.

"I was thinking maybe you wouldn't make it this morning," he says. He doesn't smile at me. He has a very charming smile—I know this quite well—but he doesn't seem inclined to aim it at me very often. But he's not as rude and resentful as he was the first day, so I have to assume he doesn't mind my presence as much as he initially indicated.

I don't mind his either, as long as he doesn't start babbling to me all the time.

"Why would you assume I wouldn't make it?" I ask, arranging my skirt around my legs. I wear a long, flowing, casual skirt—the kind I used to wear all the time. It feels like me, so I'm glad I put it on this morning.

"You weren't here when I got here."

"I'm here at my normal time. You're here earlier than usual."

He looks at his watch, as if surprised. "Am I?"

"Yes."

"I lose track of time sometimes."

I wonder if this is true—and, if so, how much it

affects him. It's a common thing to happen once a person hits seventy. Dave seems to be in quite good shape physically. He can walk and dance and play tennis a lot better than I possibly could. But there must be a reason he moved from the independent-living cottages to the assisted-living residence last year.

Maybe it's his memory.

If so, it's certainly not debilitating, since this is the first time I've noticed any sign of it.

"Well, it's just after six thirty in the morning right now," I say. "This is the time I always get here."

"You always leave at the same time?"

"Yes. Give or take a few minutes. Why?"

"I was just wondering if you still live by a schedule."

Of course I live by a schedule. I go to bed around the same time every night. I wake up around the same time too. I eat breakfast at seven and lunch at eleven thirty, tea around three and dinner by five thirty. I leave for my walk at about a quarter after six.

Even after a week at Eagle's Rest, my schedule has been finalized. When I was younger—when I was working—my schedule each day would often look different, since I could never predict what might come up throughout the day.

But now, nothing ever comes up. Days fall into a familiar rhythm. There is security in that. Comfort.

I know I'm not the only person my age who has found the same thing to be true.

I imagine Dave is not much different.

"Don't you?" I ask, lifting my eyebrows in the way I always do when I want to convey mild irony.

"Yes," he admits. "Most of the time. Sometimes it's damned boring."

Maybe it is, but it doesn't bother me. I never get bored.

"What?" he asks, after a moment, as if he can see I have something in mind, something I might say.

I'm not usually inclined to share what I'm thinking with people—certainly not with a man who is a virtual stranger. But I hear myself saying anyway, "I was just thinking that I don't get bored. Even with the same schedule every day, I can always find something to entertain myself."

He's peering at me again, turning his head so he can see my expression. "What do you do to entertain yourself?"

I'm surprised by the question, since the answer should be obvious. "I think. I read. I do word games. I watch movies. I walk. I look out onto Valentine Valley."

He turns his head toward the valley, and he asks in a different tone, "What do you see there?"

I give a little shrug, feeling strangely jittery, although there's absolutely no reason for it. "Home."

The answer seems to affect him, since he's still and silent for nearly a full minute. Then he finally murmurs, "Yes. That's something, isn't it?"

We don't talk again until we leave to walk back. I get up first, and he follows.

The following day, I go to a yoga class with Marjorie.

When she first invited me to go, I laughed, telling her that simply walking is hard enough for me. Standing on my hands will be impossible.

"Oh, but it's chair yoga," she says. "None of us can do the fancy moves, but I'm sure you'll like it. All the ladies from the knitting circle go."

I've never heard of chair yoga, but Marjorie is much frailer than I am. If she can do it, then surely I can too. I like Marjorie—more every time we talk—and I prefer to say yes to her if I can.

So I change into a long T-shirt and stretchy pants that Beth has always called "yoga pants." Surely that's an appropriate outfit for chair yoga. I pull my hair back in a ponytail so it won't get in the way.

I don't have nearly the energy I used to. Every time I try to do something active now, it takes a concerted effort to start. But I'm usually pleased with myself after it's done—proud that I accomplished something—so I hope I'll feel the same way after this class.

Evidently, chair yoga is done while sitting in a straight-backed chair. There are fifteen of them lined up in a room in the community center with a wall of mirrors. The teacher is the peppy staff member who is in charge of health activities for the residents. She's a little too peppy for my taste. There's only so long a person can smile before I start to believe that it's fake.

But Marjorie is thrilled that I'm here, so I'm glad I made myself come. I sit in the chair next to her, and she tells me the names of all the women in her knitting circle.

Some of them I've met already, and the others I recognize from around the residence. Marjorie tells me little details about them—"Stella has had four husbands, you know"—"Mary can't drink milk or anything dairy. It makes her gassy"—"Clarisse keeps a thousand dollars in cash under her mattress"—and she speaks so loudly that all of the women must be able to hear her.

They either smile in fond amusement or give her annoyed glances over their shoulders. This gives me a clue about whether they're the kind of women I will like.

The class begins, and we all have to stretch our arms in various positions, breathe deeply, and keep our posture very straight. It's really not so bad. The stretching actually feels good. And it might even be relaxing were not all the women having conversations with each other while they performed the moves.

It seems like yoga should be a quieter activity,

but the peppy class leader doesn't even try to shush anyone. She's probably used to it.

Marjorie tells me about the dance lessons she had as a child. Evidently, she was really good at ballroom dancing and got to perform at some fancy hotels. She lived in a number of big cities after she got married, and for a while she still tried to keep up her dancing. It's interesting to listen to her. She's had such a different life than I have. I wonder if she regrets giving up dancing, but she never says anything that makes me think so.

The chair yoga class goes quickly, and I've actually enjoyed myself. As we leave the room, I thank Marjorie for inviting me.

"Oh, did I invite you, dear?" she asks.

She's definitely a little spacey, but it's very clear to me now that it has nothing to do with her intelligence or her heart. I'm glad to have met her. I would even call her a friend.

"You did." I feel a wave of affection and do something that's not something I often do. I lean over and kiss her on the cheek. "It was a lovely thing to do."

She smiles, clearly pleased by the gesture.

As I straighten up, I see a couple of men walking down the hall, dressed like they've been playing tennis.

One of them is Dave. I recognize him well before I'm able to make out his features. His body, his stride, is unmistakable.

At least to me.

He's watching me as he approaches, and I see something like curiosity in his eyes.

For a moment, I wonder how I look, in the baggy T-shirt and ponytail. Then I remind myself that it really doesn't matter.

He nods politely, and the man with him tells both Marjorie and me hello. Then they've walked past us and the encounter is over.

I feel vaguely disappointed, but I'm not sure what else I expected. Dave and I aren't friends.

We just aren't.

"He has eyes for you," Marjorie says.

I turn toward her quickly. "What do you mean?"

"Dave Andrews. He has eyes for you."

"He does not. He barely acknowledged us."

She gives a tittering laugh and doesn't say any more, but I wonder if she's seen more in him than I did.

It's Thursday before I decide to ask Dave the question I've wanted to ask each morning.

We've seen each other every day, sitting on the bench together. We always have a brief conversation, but it never lasts very long.

We're not friends. We're not close. We're still mostly strangers—strangers who share a few minutes together, cut off from the rest of the world, here on the edge of the mountain.

On Thursday, he's complaining about his arm, which he evidently pulled the other day playing tennis. I tell him he should be more careful, since he's not a young man anymore.

He doesn't appreciate this comment. He sits in silence for a few minutes with a frown on his face.

At first, I'm amused, since I knew what his reaction would be to my words and said them anyway. But then I feel more confident, as if Dave isn't quite so distant and foreign as he felt a few days ago. So I consider the possibility for a few minutes before I ask, "Who is Clara?"

Dave gives a little jerk, startled either by my voice or by the question itself. "What's that?"

"Who is Clara?" I repeat. I'm quite sure he heard the question the first time, but this is something that I do too when I'm taken off guard—use a clarifying question to give myself a little time to find more secure footing.

"Oh." He looks away.

Well, it's obvious he doesn't want to talk about her, but I want to know, and I'm not going to back down now that I've asked. It would make me look weak and spineless. "Was she your wife?"

"No." He meets my eyes again, and there's a challenge in his expression that I'm not expecting. "She was my daughter."

"Oh." I swallow, feeling a little wave of guilt at bringing up a subject that must be painful to him. "She died?" There would be no reason for a memorial bench to the girl if she were still living.

"Yes."

"When was that?" He didn't have kids when I knew him back at the college, so he must have had the girl when he was in his late forties or fifties. Not unusual, for men.

"She was only thirteen. It's been a long time."

"That's so sad. What happened to her?"

He'd looked reluctant to talk about it at first, but now he answers easily, as if he's released a breath or let something go—something that allows him to open up. "Leukemia. She fought it for four years."

"Wow. That's . . ." Heartbreaking.

"There are no words. I know." He's not looking at me, but it doesn't feel like he's closing me out. I don't know why I'm surprised that he's faced a tragedy like this in his life—everyone has their share of heartaches if they reach the age we are—but I am surprised. His life has always seemed charmed to me. Easy.

But I should know better by now.

I should know better.

"Was your wife still around when it happened?" I don't actually know the full story with his wife, so I try to be careful with the words.

He nods. "We divorced after she died. It was like

we couldn't stand to even look at each other anymore. I guess that's normal." He leans back against the bench, stretching out his legs.

"I heard your wife died."

He looks surprised for just a moment. "Oh, you must mean my second wife. She died, yes. About nine years ago, before I moved here."

"Do you have any other children?"

"No."

I remember what Charlotte told me. "Stepchildren, then?"

"Yes, I have a whole passel of stepkids." He shakes his head. "Not the same."

"No," I say. "I guess not." The stepkids would have been older when he married his second wife. Even if his wife was a lot younger than him, they would probably have at least been teenagers. It might have been hard to bond in a situation like that.

"You never had kids?" he asks, his expression changing, as if he's putting the sad stuff behind him.

I know the feeling. I experience it more and more as I get older. There's simply too much that hurts, too much to dwell on. You have to think of other things if you're to make yourself keep going.

Onward, as Gordon said on Saturday night.

"No, I never had kids."

"Did you want them?" It's a presumptuous question, but I've been asking him presumptuous questions too, so I can hardly resent it.

I shake my head. "No. I never really did. There was a time, when I was younger, when I wouldn't have minded having kids. But when I finally had the chance, it just didn't feel right."

"Hmm."

I figure that's response enough, so I stare out to the valley once more. The sun is bright today, and it's flashing against the water of the lake in the distance.

"I have a very good nephew," I say after a moment of silence. "He and his youngest daughter are very good to me."

Dave's forehead wrinkles, and for a moment he looks almost bleak. "That's good. You aren't alone."

I don't like that flicker of emotion I catch on his face, so I say something in an attempt to be positive. "And you have your stepkids. Someone said you went on vacation with them, so I guess they take good care of you."

Dave gives a slightly bitter laugh. "Oh, yes."

I don't know what he means by that, but it worries me.

That afternoon, I have tea with Charlotte.

I don't see Charlotte every day, since sometimes she's busy and sometimes she's off duty. But I like her the best of all the staff at Eagle's Rest I've met so far, and I'm pleased when she comes over to sit with me on the veranda where I'm drinking my tea.

We're chatting lightly about books we've read and places we've traveled when I see her eyes drift away from me.

Long experience has taught me what that means, so I turn my head automatically to see what has distracted her.

I see Gayle Langston, who is the managing director of this community. I've only met her once in person, but I see her around quite a bit. She's a middle-aged professional woman who comes across as efficient and no-nonsense.

With her is a man I've never seen before. He wears good trousers and a white dress shirt, and he's probably in his forties—with a high forehead and a sharp chin. I recognize that a lot of women would find him attractive, but I've never liked his kind of looks.

I turn back to Charlotte and see that her eyes are fixed on the man. He glances over at us and gives a wave and a smile in our direction.

Charlotte waves back, her cheeks flushing as she giggles.

This must be Kevin, the lawyer.

"Is that someone important?" I ask.

"It's Kevin," she says, giving me a look I well recognize, that secretly excited look that girls get when they want to confess something juicy. "Dave

Andrews is his stepfather, so he comes out occasionally to look in on him. He's good about that kind of thing."

"Is he? He should come over and talk with you then."

Charlotte shakes her head and watches as Kevin parts with Gayle and walks away, not giving us even a second glance. "He's very professional. He doesn't do that kind of thing."

"Oh. I see." Although I don't see at all. After a moment, I watch a very expensive red sports car drive down the road that leads out of the property. "Is that him?"

"Yes. Isn't it a beautiful car?"

"I guess. He must have a lucrative practice."

"He does very well, I think. And with Dave as his stepfather, there's family money."

"I see." I want to say more. I want to tell her not to be silly, not to put her hopes in a man who will never fulfill her dreams. I can see it so clearly. Kevin might be spending some time with Charlotte, but it's not because he's serious about her. A man who is even halfway interested would have stopped by our table to say hello, at least.

I've always hated when I see women doing this—placing their faith in men who will never live up to that faith. I did so myself a few times, and I well remember the emotional limbo, the will-he-won't-he angst that always led to deep disappointment.

I don't want that for Charlotte, but there's nothing for me to do. If I give her advice at this point she'll only reject it and probably cool off toward me.

Unfortunately, what I want to tell her can only be learned through experience.

Charlotte must be forty or close to it, but not every woman has a lot of romantic experiences early.

And some women want a man so much they forget what their experiences have taught them.

"It's really too bad," Charlotte says, leaning closer to me, as if she has a different sort of secret to share.

"What is?"

"I guess that Kevin's brother and sisters are being rather greedy about Dave's money."

My eyes widen, genuinely surprised. "Are they? What are they doing?"

"I'm not quite sure. It's just a few things that Kevin has said. Dave made a lot of money in his life. I suppose you might know that, if you knew him before."

"Yes, I'm not surprised by that."

"And, since he has no children, I guess some of his stepkids take advantage of him."

"Do they expect to inherit when he dies?"

"I guess they do. I don't know any details, but I think Kevin is worried by it. He's a good guy."

I'm not sure about that, but I'm not prepared to completely dismiss it, either. Kevin might be a good guy. Good guys certainly have been known to lead women on. They do it all the time, often completely obliviously.

I've decided I don't like Kevin, but that doesn't mean he's a grasping stepson.

I certainly hope not. I'd like to think that at least one of Dave's stepsons cares enough about him to prefer him alive rather than dead.

six

*W*hen I worked in the college library, I used to have lunch in the main dining hall nearly every day. Sometimes I would sit with other members of the staff, but often I would eat alone.

I enjoyed those lunches the best.

I'd watch the students as they came and went, eating their meals and talking to each other. Some of the students I knew by name from time they'd spent in the library, but most I only knew by sight. I'd watch relationships formed, rivalries solidified, hearts broken—all over sandwiches, salads, pizza, cereal, and a variety of bland main dishes. I'd witness the entire arc of romances, from first meeting to intense passion to awkward distance after a breakup.

I never got tired of observing the students' lives as they were played out while eating lunch.

I'm starting to get the same feeling here at Eagle's Rest.

There are fifty-eight residents who live in the main building. By my second week, I recognize most of them and know about half of them by name, although I've only spoken to twenty or so. I'm certainly familiar enough with them now to know which of them love each other, which hate each other, which have some sort of personal history, and which hang out together because there's no one else.

There are two rivals for Dave's attention, although several other women would jump if he called. But the two residents who appear most competitive over him—who believe they have the most hope—are Gladys and Kathy.

Gladys is the bleached blonde he was dancing with on Saturday. She's a little larger than me and always wears the most ridiculous high heels. I've never been a fan—even back when I was younger and they might have been appropriate—but I'd never dream of wearing heels that high now. Gladys does every day, and she wobbles around in an almost laughable way. I'm surprised she doesn't break an ankle, since she doesn't seem steady on her feet even without the heels. She manages, although it takes her longer to get from place to place than it takes me—even with my walker.

Kathy is a redhead who is always dressed to the nines. She was dancing with Dave on Saturday night too. Her shoes are always more reasonable than Gladys's, but she must spend an hour doing her makeup every morning. Sometimes I stare at her cheekbones and eyelids, as if they are works of art. I don't find the overall effect particularly flattering, but the male residents seem to appreciate it.

There's a kind of competition between Gladys and

Kathy at mealtimes. I noticed it early on. They both plant themselves at tables on opposite sides of the dining room—I'm sure they consider them "their" tables—and wait to see which one Dave will sit at.

He usually sits with one or the other of them, but there's no clear pattern or method to which he'll choose. Occasionally, he sits at an entirely different table in the room.

He never sits at mine.

At lunch on Thursday, the following week, I'm eating my vegetable soup and crusty bread when I see him arrive. He looks a little windblown, like he's spent most of the morning outside. I have no idea what he does between breakfast and lunch, since I always go back to my apartment.

His dark eyes scan the room, as they always do. It wouldn't be unreasonable for him to decide to join me. Early this morning, we spent more than a half hour together on the bench, talking about the schools we attended as children. It was the most extended and convivial conversation we've ever had, and I enjoyed it far more than I would have expected.

In a normal situation, Dave might come to join me for lunch, but I'm neither surprised nor disappointed when he doesn't.

Our time on the bench doesn't feel like it's part of the real world. It feels isolated, cut off, distanced from what we do and who we are at the residence.

After all, we're not friends. We're just two people

who share a bench every morning, since it's the place both of us want to be.

I would never dream of going over there to chat with him, and I'm sure he feels the same way about me.

Dave eats his meals with Gladys or Kathy—and whoever else happens to be at their tables. He doesn't eat his meals with me.

I'm sitting with Marjorie and Gordon, who have become my regular mealtime companions. We talked about the soup and about plans for the afternoon—tea on the veranda as usual, except Marjorie's daughter is coming by to take her out to the salon to get her hair done. At the moment, we're just sitting quietly.

I'm watching as Dave's eyes scan my side of the room and come to rest briefly on me. Our eyes meet for a moment, but then his gaze passes on, and he heads over to Gladys's table.

It doesn't feel like a rejection, even though it could have been. It feels more like an acknowledgment that I exist.

I feel an unfamiliar stirring of excitement—somewhere in the vicinity of my breastbone. He's never acknowledged I exist in the dining room before.

Gordon obviously noticed our brief gaze. He nods over toward Dave as he sits down next to Gladys, who is brimming with excitement as she always does on days he chooses her. "I heard his shyster stepson is trying to get him to change the will."

I put down my spoon and straighten up. "Kevin, you mean? The young man Charlotte is seeing?"

"Is she dating him? I wouldn't have thought she was his type."

I don't actually think she is his type, but that's not an appropriate topic for today. "I heard that Kevin was trying to protect Dave from the clutches of his brother and sisters."

Gordon frowns. "Maybe. That's not what I heard, though."

"Who did you hear it from?"

"I don't remember. Someone was talking about it."

That's not particularly helpful information for me. I'd really like to know whether Kevin is out to help or hurt Dave, but there doesn't seem to be anyone from whom I can get a straight answer.

I'd have to talk to Kevin myself and try to get a good read on him, but there's not likely to be an opportunity for me to do so.

"I'm sure Dave can take care of himself," I murmur, watching him as he listens to whatever Gladys is chattering about. "He's not a pushover."

"It's not always that easy," Gordon says, and I know he's right.

Things that seem obvious and easy when you're younger—like managing your finances and making your own decisions—aren't always as easy or even possible at our age.

Sometimes it's because of our own limitations, and sometimes it's because others think we're helpless.

There's something that bothers me unduly about the idea of Dave being taken advantage of, and it's not only for the obvious reason—that I don't think he should be hurt. It's also because I remember him as so strong and willful and powerful. He could get anyone to do what he wanted, and he never caved to anyone else's will.

The possibility that he's changed—that he's not as strong as he used to be—unsettles me, makes my belly roll in an uncomfortable way.

Kind of like seeing a beautiful medieval text faded and crumbling or watching a gorgeous, historic church get torn down.

The good things in this world should last a little longer, and it's wrong when they don't.

I wonder if Dave will ever choose between Gladys and Kathy. Maybe he should, so he doesn't keep stringing both of them along.

They seem to enjoy the drama, though. Kathy is over on the far side of the room, sending pouting glances to the other table and flirting with Laird Draycott, who is likely proposing to her at this very moment.

Dave was right. This place feels more like school

every day. I suppose people are the same, no matter what their age. Put them all in the same place, and every flavor of human drama will be played out, no matter how small the space.

I look back toward Dave and see his eyes are resting on me.

I wonder if I should smile, but I don't. I don't want anyone to notice me smiling at him.

When I was a girl, I was terrified of anyone ever finding out about the men I was interested in. It felt like weakness, like vulnerability—admitting I wanted a romantic attachment.

I guess I haven't really changed.

The next morning I walk out the back door of the building and through the gardens on my way to the path around the woods.

I stop in surprise when I see Dave, standing just where the lawn ends and the woods begin.

He's facing in my direction, and he appears to be waiting for me.

I continue walking as soon as I process his appearance, but my heart is beating unusually fast. It's silly, of course. He probably just happened to see me leave the building and paused out of general politeness.

It's not like he would have made a point of waiting around so he could walk to the bench with me.

That's not likely at all.

"I saw you come out," he says as I approach him, confirming my suspicion that it's just civility and happenstance.

"It's warm this morning," I say, as he falls in step with me. "Humid." The feeling of fall from last week is gone. It's like summer again.

"Yes."

"I don't like it."

"You'll be complaining about the cold soon enough," he says, a dry humor in his tone.

This is true of most people, but it's not true of me, and I tell him so. "I never complain about the cold. I'd much rather it be cold than warm."

"Most people change their mind about that when they get older."

I shake my head. "Not me. I do get colder than I used to get, but I've never liked the summer, and I still don't."

"So you don't like to vacation in tropical places, then?"

"I've been to Hawaii once and the Caribbean a couple of times, and I enjoyed them just fine. But that's because the whole trip is centered around the beach and pools. I certainly wouldn't want to live somewhere like that."

"What was your favorite vacation in your life?"

It's strange how quickly you can grow comfortable with someone. Two weeks ago, I didn't know or like

Dave Andrews. Now, however, it's normal for him to ask me these kinds of questions, and I actually enjoy answering them, since it feels like he's really listening to me.

"My friends and I went to England in our twenties," I say, smiling at the memory. "Oh, we had a grand time."

"Have you never been back, then?"

"Oh, yes, I've been back several times. I always enjoyed it, but it never quite equals the first time, does it?"

His thick eyebrows draw together, as if he's considering this idea. "Maybe not."

"What about you?"

"What about me?"

I frown up at him, since he seems to do this a lot, hem and haw when the conversation turns back to him. "What was your favorite vacation?"

"I don't really know."

We've reached the bench now, so I move my walker to the side and sit down, wincing slightly as my knee gives a throb of pain.

There's nothing particularly wrong with my knee, other than old age and arthritis, so it's just one of those pains you get used to.

"You must remember at least one vacation you really enjoyed," I prompt, not wanting him to back out of answering the question.

"There were a lot of them." He's staring off at the

distance now, the way he does when he's searching his mind, searching his memory. "When Clara was nine, her mother and I took her to Florida to go to Disney World and Sea World and that whole lot. She had so much fun."

"I bet she did. And that's the one you remember the most?" I kind of like that about him—that the vacation that resonates most with him is the one his daughter most enjoyed. It says something about him I wouldn't have realized a week ago.

"It was just before she was diagnosed."

My heart does a painful twist, and I let out a long breath. "Can you look back on the good memories now and . . . and be happy?"

He turns his head to meet my eyes, and there's something in his face that is open, genuine—something that makes my heartbeat speed up just a little bit. "Yeah. Usually, I can."

"That's good."

We sit in silence for several minutes, but it doesn't feel awkward or lonely. Both of us seem content with our thoughts, and I'm actually glad to have him there. As if there can be companionship in presence alone.

"Did you enjoy Niagara Falls?" I ask, finally breaking the silence as the question pops into my head.

I don't usually speak the first thing that enters my thoughts, so I'm not sure why I did just then.

He blinks a couple of times and turns to look at me. "It was okay."

"Just okay? Had you been there before?"

"No."

"We went once when I was a girl. I remember enjoying going out in that boat."

"Yes. We did the boat. It was . . . fine."

He seems stiffer than he did before, but I don't think it's because he's annoyed or impatient with me. I think it has to do with something else. I want to know for sure, so I say lightly, "It was nice of your stepkids to take you."

He clears his throat and arches his eyebrows. "I suppose."

This is getting closer to what I want to know, but I have to be careful or he'll close down the conversation. "What was the trip for? Someone's birthday or a celebration of some kind?"

"I don't know." He sounds almost tired now. "Kevin, one of the boys, just came up with the idea of us going on vacation, and then they all piled on. Both girls have husbands and one of them has a couple of kids, so it ended up being a big crew."

"Whose idea was it to go to Niagara Falls?"

"Who knows?"

"Did you not want to go there?" I ask, responding to the slight bitterness in his tone.

"Not really. I'd have chosen somewhere else."

"Then why didn't you tell them that?"

He gives a slight shrug and half smiles at me. "Why bother?"

"What do you mean?"

"I mean it's not worth the effort. If they want to go to Niagara, why argue?"

I'm starting to understand something—a conclusion that pieces together the various bits I've been noticing over the last two weeks. It's not that Dave has really gotten weak-willed in his old age. It's that he just doesn't want to make the effort anymore.

As if it's just not worth it to put up a fight.

Things always came easy for him when he was younger. He was the center of attention without even trying. People scurried to do his will with very little work on his part. Maybe that makes it harder, now that he's older, now that it doesn't happen so easily.

"If you wanted something else, it might be worth it."

He keeps watching me, and his expression becomes almost curious. I much prefer this expression, even though he's obviously searching my face, trying to discover my thoughts. "Do you think so?"

"Of course I think so. Why wouldn't it be worth it?"

"It's a lot of work, fighting a losing battle."

I frown. "Why is the battle losing?"

"When you're our age? How can the battle not be losing?"

I know exactly what he means, and I can't even

really argue with the point. It takes energy and will and effort to hold out against resistance, and most of that energy for us is spent going through the basic routine of living.

"It's just a vacation," he adds, more softly now. "What does it matter?"

"Do you like your stepchildren?" I ask, knowing very well that the question is a risk.

He gives another shrug. "They're the only family I have anymore."

That might be true, but it doesn't answer my question.

Every day for the next week, when I walk outside in the mornings, Dave is waiting for me on the path at the end of the garden.

The first couple of times, it could have been chance, but by the third morning there was no way to deny it was intentional. He was waiting for me so he could walk to the bench with me.

We walk back together too.

Every morning as I got dressed, I felt a rising of jittery excitement, wondering if he would be there waiting, wondering what we would say to each other, wondering if he was looking forward to it like I was.

I spent the rest of the day looking forward to the following morning.

When I was thirty, I was in graduate school, and I fell desperately in love with a fellow student. He was a few years younger than me, but he was deliciously handsome, with thick blond hair and the artistically sculpted features of a Romantic poet—maybe Byron or Shelley.

His name was Mat—with only one *t*.

We met in a couple of classes we took together, and we started grabbing a cup of coffee after class. Every morning, I spent ridiculous amounts of time dressing attractively and planning out things to say that would impress or amuse him. He never called me or asked me out on a date, but I was sure he was falling for me as much as I was falling for him.

Oh, the daydreams I had of our future—courtship, wedding, honeymoon, an adorable cottage in the woods where we would grow old together, complete with rose garden and arbor. I had the whole span of our lives planned out in my mind, based on nothing but coffee and casual conversation.

I was thirty then, but I could still be silly. Particularly over men.

He liked me well enough, and he enjoyed hanging out with me. He wasn't romantically interested in me at all, though.

I sighed after him for an entire semester, until I had to admit there was nothing there. I think I must have gotten too forward with him, because he gradually became more distant, more elusive, until the semester ended and that was it.

He wasn't in any of my classes the following semester, and I only saw him once or twice in passing. He barely even acknowledged me.

I'm convinced he wasn't an asshole. Not really. He was just hanging out with me because it was easy and enjoyable and he didn't realize or didn't care that it was generating unrealistic hopes in me.

I wonder, on Friday morning, after two weeks of spending time with Dave on the bench, if I'm doing the same thing now.

Maybe, at age seventy-one, I'm not any wiser about men.

I'm not daydreaming about Dave, though. I'm looking forward to our mornings at the bench, and that's all. I don't really have expectations of anything else happening between us.

He has Gladys and Kathy, after all, and he still doesn't do more than nod at me at other times of the day.

He's enjoying our mornings together as much as I am. If he weren't, he wouldn't be waiting for me on the path every day. It isn't foolish to enjoy it, and to enjoy the fact that he wants to spend time with me.

I'm not expecting anything else.

Honestly, I'm not sure what else there could be.

I feel the same acceleration of my heart, however,

as I walk out the door on that Friday morning. I'm a couple of minutes later than usual because I spilled my leftover tea as I was putting it in the sink and didn't want to leave before I cleaned it up.

Dave should be waiting for me.

I hope he is.

I let out a breath of relief as I see him standing in his normal place. He's looking down at the paved path, frowning.

I wave as he looks up, and I see his face change.

"You're late," he says, as I reach him.

Now, it's my turn to frown. "Just a couple of minutes."

"Five minutes."

"I'm sorry. I had a slight accident with my tea and had to do some cleanup. You could have gone on without me, if you were getting impatient."

"I thought maybe you weren't going to come today."

There's no way for me to deny the flicker of pleasure I feel at the realization that this idea bothers him—the possibility that I wasn't going to turn up for our morning walk. He was worried about it. That's why he was frowning when I first saw him.

"I always come," I say, making sure to sound as composed as I always do. "I never miss my walk."

"Good."

We walk up to the bench, making an occasional comment about the weather or the state of our knees this morning. Then, when we reach the bench, we fall into that companionable silence I most enjoy as we both watch a couple of squirrels scampering around in the grass and the few leaves that are starting to fall.

"Oh, look," I say, after several minutes. "He's found something."

Dave has leaned over to peer at the squirrel in question. "What is it? A piece of bread?"

"I think it's a piece of donut," I say, after my own examination. "Someone must have dropped it yesterday. Look how proud he is of it."

Dave and I chuckle as we watch the squirrel lord his find over the other one.

"My dogs used to chase squirrels," I say, smiling at so many memories. "The squirrels would always run up trees, and then they'd hang out in the branches, teasing the poor dogs. I'm sure they would do it on purpose."

"Which of your dogs?" he asks. I've mentioned my dogs a couple of times before, so he knows I've had several in my life.

"All of them. They were all Spaniels, and they all saw squirrels as enemies that needed to be vanquished. Alcott, my last dog, used to try to jump up after them in the trees. She was able to balance on her hind legs for several seconds as she tried to reach them." My smile fades a little as I think about my dear brown cocker spaniel, who died only a few months ago.

The memory hits me hard for some reason, and my eyes start to burn.

I glance away, strangely embarrassed.

Dave doesn't say anything, although I know he must notice my reaction.

After a minute, he reaches over and picks up my hand, which has been resting on the bench beside me. He holds my hand in his in a comforting gesture that can't possibly be mistaken.

I'm surprised—very surprised—but I don't pull my hand away. I don't want to pull it away. His hand is wrinkled, like mine, and he has more age spots on his skin than I do. But his hand is warm and dry, and it feels solid. Secure.

I can't remember the last time I've touched another person like this, in more than a casual gesture. It warms something inside me—the knowledge that Dave is here, he understands how I feel about Alcott, he wants me to feel better.

We sit on the bench together in silence for a long time, holding hands. He occasionally strokes the back of my hand with his thumb, but just lightly and not in a way that feels intrusive or annoying.

It feels nice. Really nice.

I'm almost embarrassed by how much I enjoy it, how I feel a little breathless as I sit beside him.

It seems like this sort of thing should feel different as you get older, but it doesn't.

It really doesn't.

seven

*I*n the afternoon, I stop by Marjorie's room, since she wasn't at breakfast or lunch. It's strange for me not to see her at all during a day. I'm a little worried about her failure to appear.

I have to knock twice before I get an answer, and then it's just a faint sound of her voice, telling me to come in from inside.

I open the door and walk into an apartment that is set up very similarly to mine—only Marjorie doesn't have the corner with windows on two walls or a patio.

It feels strange and unnerving to walk into a dark room in the middle of the afternoon. It feels off, wrong, with all the blinds closed and none of the lamps or overhead lights on.

"Oh dear," I say, walking farther in and seeing that Marjorie is lying in bed under the covers. "Are you sick?"

"Just not feeling up to snuff today," she says with a fluttery smile. She's very pale. I can see it even in the darkened room. "It's so kind of you to come visit."

"I was wondering about you, since you didn't show up for breakfast or lunch." I glance around and see a small side chair against a wall, so I drag it over close enough to her bed so I can sit down and talk to her. "Do you think you have a virus or something?"

She shakes her head, her fluffy white hair brushing against her skin. "It's just my heart. It's always giving me problems."

I feel a drop in my belly at hearing this. I hadn't realized that Marjorie has heart problems, and they're likely to be more serious than a short-lived bug. "Have you seen the doctor?"

"Charlotte said he'll be by this afternoon, and she'll make sure he looks in on me. It's that very nice Dr. Martin."

"I don't think I know him."

"He comes by every week." Her mood seems as light and scattered as it always does, but she's breathless and has to pause occasionally between words. "He has a lot of patients here, and he's so good about checking on us. He's such a kind, quiet man. You'll like him."

"I'm sure I will. He sounds like a very good doctor, to come out here to see his patients."

"Gladys is his patient too. She had to see him last week."

"Did she? She didn't look sick." Maybe it was her ankles, troubling her from always wearing such ridiculously high heels.

Marjorie lifts her head up a little and then says in a stage whisper. "Female troubles."

My eyebrows go up high. In my day, any number of ailments might be labeled female troubles, from PMS to an unwanted pregnancy. But surely none of those particular conditions could possibly apply to Gladys. So, maybe it's nosy—it is most certainly nosy—but I ask anyway, since I want to know. "What kind of female troubles?"

I keep my voice down out of respect for Marjorie's sensibilities, not because of any of my own. I've never been embarrassed by sex or the basics of biology —not since I was a teenager.

"Oh, I don't know," she replies, shaking her head in concern. "Some sort of infection, I believe. She's been . . ." Marjorie clears her throat. "She's been *at it,* I believe."

I'm already feeling kind of low, since Marjorie is clearly so ill. This news, however, causes my gut to twist into a painful knot.

Gladys has been *at it*.

I can't help but wonder who she's been at it with.

I'm not naive. I'm not even close. I know very well that many of the residents here are having sex. Ever since those little pills for men became readily available, sex as a common activity for seniors has been back on the table.

So to speak. Most of us wouldn't be limber enough to do much on an actual table.

I can look around at mealtimes and pick out couples that I'm quite sure are sexually intimate, and others I suspect—even some that haven't even identified themselves as couples.

But I never thought it might be true of Dave and

any of the women here. I certainly haven't seen any clear signs of such a thing, and I don't like the idea that he's been having sex with Gladys.

Not just because I don't think she's right for him at all. But also because, if he has been having sex, then he's been stringing her along in a rather heartless way.

She obviously wants to be paired up with him, but he has done nothing obvious to confirm that they're a couple. If they're having sex, however, then there's every reason for Gladys to think they *should* be a couple.

I have no doubt that casual sex happens at any age and stage of life, but there's no way in the world that Gladys wants to be casual. She wants to be with Dave for real. I suddenly feel sorry for Gladys, with her bleached hair and vaginal infection.

I really hope Dave hasn't been taking advantage of her feelings.

I can't respect a man who does that, no matter how desperately he wants to reclaim the virility of his youth. I just can't.

"Oh," I say, since clearly I need to respond in some way to what Marjorie has told me. I clear my throat. "I'm surprised she talks about it, since it seems like a private matter."

"It should be." Marjorie is shaking her head. "It should be, but you know how things are here. She's kind of a show-off, and she was hinting at it the other day during our bridge game."

"I see. Did she give any hint about who her partner has been?"

Maybe it's wrong of me to ask, but if it's Dave, I want to hear it straight out, so I'll know what to think.

"Oh, you know how she is."

I do know how she is, but this doesn't give me an answer at all. So I ask more directly, "Is it Dave Andrews, do you think?"

Marjorie's eyes go as round as saucers. "Dave? Oh, no, I don't think so. She wants him, but she doesn't have him. Dave has eyes for you."

My relief is palpable, and it's rather worrying, since I shouldn't care so much about what Dave does. So he held my hand this morning. That doesn't mean anything, necessarily.

"Gladys spends time with Milton Collier, so that's who I believe it must be. I don't understand what they're thinking." Marjorie is still shaking her head, clearly baffled by such goings-on.

Milton Collier I've seen but never met. He reminds me of a peacock, always strutting and puffing out his chest and trying to make a lot out of himself. His being with Gladys in that way makes a lot more sense to me than her with Dave. That story rings true, and I genuinely believe it's not just because I want it to be true.

Since Marjorie is waiting for a response from me, I say softly, "I guess, when folks are our age, they want to grab hold of life, in any way they can."

"I suppose. I just think there are easier and less messy ways to grab hold of life." Marjorie looked faintly disgusted.

In the times I had a partner, I had a pretty good sex life—one I enjoyed—but I know that's not true of all women. Maybe it's not true of Marjorie. Or, maybe, like me, she just feels too tired most of the time to even think about having sex anymore.

"Anyway," I say, deciding to change the subject. I shouldn't be feeding my own curiosity when Marjorie isn't feeling well. "We should talk of something more pleasant, to perk you up a little."

"Oh, yes," she says. "I'd love to be perked up." She looks very old and very pale and very tired. I'm suddenly scared for her. "Do you like to knit?"

I smile as I tell her I don't. We have a light conversation about the various things she's knitted in her life until there's a light tap on the door.

Charlotte comes in with a balding, middle-aged man. I remember him from the day I arrived here. He held the door open for me with such a nice smile.

This is evidently Dr. Martin, whom Charlotte calls John.

I offer to leave, but Marjorie doesn't want me to, so I move away from the bed as he chats with her and examines her.

He's the sort of man I would want for a doctor. He's got the most soothing, gentle voice, and his brown eyes are so sincerely warm. He's probably close to fifty, and he's lost at least half his hair, but I really like his face—as much as I like his manner.

"It's really nice of him to come out to see patients here," I say to Charlotte. Both of us are standing in the living room area so we don't intrude.

"Yes. He's always done it, ever since I started working here. He goes to see some of his patients in town too, if they can't get out to come to the office for him."

"How generous he must be."

"He's a good guy." Charlotte is smiling in his direction, with genuine appreciation. It's not anything like the look I saw her give to Kevin last week, but it suddenly sparks an idea.

"Is he married?" I ask. I'm an old lady. I can ask those kinds of things without people thinking I'm rude.

Charlotte shakes her head. "No."

"I would think a lot of women would be looking in his direction, then."

She looks surprised. "Oh, I don't think so. I wouldn't know, though. Maybe they do."

She's shrugged off Dr. Martin as if he is of no interest to her, other than being a good doctor for the residents here. It bothers me that she's done so, even though I know very well that I did the same thing when I was her age and younger.

I can look back and pinpoint several good men I never gave a second thought to—all of whom would have made excellent husbands and partners.

I feel kind of down as I wait for him to finish up with Marjorie, and I listen as he gently tells her she might be feeling a lot better tomorrow. With her condition, she's going to have some bad days, but nothing serious seems to have changed.

I can read between the lines. She only has a certain amount of time left with her heart—so she can't expect to always feel good.

On his way out, he pauses where Charlotte and I are standing.

"Can you keep her company for a little while?" he asks me. "She's so social that having someone with her always helps her feel better."

"Yes," I say. "Of course. I'm happy to."

"Thank you. I'm sorry we haven't met before." He holds out his hand to me. "I'm John Martin. It's very nice to meet you."

I shake his hand and introduce myself and like him even more now than I did before.

I see his eyes dart over briefly to Charlotte, but he's looking down as he murmurs, "You'll call me if anything changes, Charlotte?"

"Of course," she says. "Thanks for coming out."

"Were you able to make the art exhibit in town last

weekend?" he asks. The two have obviously known each other for a while, and it seems a perfectly normal piece of casual conversation.

But I see something in how he keeps looking and then looking away from her.

Charlotte smiles at him with her normal cheerful demeanor. Nothing special. Nothing intimate. "No, I had to miss it. I was hoping—" She breaks off when a chirp from her pocket indicates she's received a text message. "Excuse me," she says, after glancing at her phone.

She turns her back on Dr. Martin and me.

When you've lived long enough, you develop a certain kind of intuition. And I know—I know as sure as anything—that the text is from Kevin.

There's a faintly wistful expression in Dr. Martin's eyes as he gives her back one last glance. Then he turns to me with another quiet smile. "Thank you for staying with her. It was very nice to meet you."

"You too." I walk with him to the door, since I want his presence to be validated. He's one of those people who fade into the background, whom others tend to overlook unless they need them.

I've sometimes felt like that myself, but I suspect he's far more that kind than I ever was.

Since shaking Charlotte by the shoulders and telling her that Dr. Martin is a far better romantic choice for her than Kevin will ever be is not really a possibility for me, there's nothing I can do but watch and wish that people were smarter.

The next morning, I'm rather distracted as I drink my tea, get dressed, and go outside to meet Dave.

I'm worried about the state of my feelings for Dave. I'm worried about Marjorie. And I'm worried about Charlotte and that sweet Dr. Martin. So I don't feel as focused or excited as I normally am while I walk through the garden.

I'm happy to see Dave, though, as he's standing there on the path at the edge of the woods. He's dressed in one of the golf shirts he normally wears and a pair of tan trousers. He's smiling as I approach him.

It's a nice smile. One that feels real. I can't help but smile back as I fall in step with him.

"You look very nice today," he says.

I glance down at myself, vaguely surprised since I didn't put much thought into my appearance earlier. I'm wearing a broomstick skirt and a tunic top with a cardigan sweater, since the morning feels a little cool. "Thank you."

I don't really need my walker anymore. I still use it, but it's mostly as a security measure. I don't lean on it anymore. I've been thinking about switching over to a cane. I'm planning to check with the doctor at my appointment on Monday to make sure that's okay.

It will be nice to put this walker away for good.

The thought of the doctor reminds me of yesterday. I really hope Marjorie is feeling better today. I'll check on her right after breakfast. She should be awake by then.

I don't really feel like talking on our walk to the bench, and Dave doesn't seem inclined to be chatty today either. It's not unusual for us to be quiet on this walk, and as we sit down next to each other at the bench, I give him a faint smile.

He must sense something in my mood, though. After a few minutes, I'm aware of him peering at me, as if he's looking for something in my face.

"What is it?" I say at last, since the silence is starting to feel uncomfortable.

"Is everything all right with you today?"

I give a little shrug. In some ways, it's unsettling—that he seems to know me so well already. But, in other ways, it's comforting. And the truth is, right now, I kind of want to tell him some of my thoughts.

"I'm just worried about Marjorie."

"Is she okay? I didn't see her yesterday."

"She wasn't feeling good and was in her bed all day. She has a bad heart. Did you know that?"

He shakes his head. "No. But it's not uncommon around here. Everyone has a bad something."

That's undeniably true.

"So is it serious?" he asks. "With Marjorie?"

"I don't know. I think it's probably serious in the long run. The doctor came out and he said nothing major has changed so it was likely just a bad day."

"Is that John Martin?"

"Yes. That's her doctor. Is he your doctor too?"

"Yes. He's good."

"He seemed like he was really nice too. I liked him."

Dave's eyebrows lift slightly. "Did you?"

"Yes. He has a really kind, gentle manner and such a nice smile."

"He seems to have made quite an impression on you, from one meeting."

"He did. I really liked him."

"What did he do to earn such favor with you?" There's a strange note in his voice, one I can't quite identify. In other circumstances, I would label it as jealous, but that's not quite right. Not here, not with us.

"He didn't do anything. He's just one of the few people I liked immediately, on first meeting, without any hesitation. It doesn't happen very often with me."

"I wouldn't think so."

"What does that mean?" I straighten my back because there's something knowing and almost smug in his voice now.

"It's not an insult. You're just the kind of person who seems to see a lot beneath the surface of people.

When you do that, it's sometimes hard to like them wholeheartedly."

I think about that. Recognize it as true. "That's true about you too, isn't it?"

"Yes. Definitely." He stares at a spot in the air for a moment. Then turns back to look at me with a half smile. "You didn't like me at first, did you?"

For some reason, I feel better now. Lighter. Still worried but not so burdened. "What makes you think I like you now?"

He obviously can see I'm teasing. "Let's just say you dislike me a little less than you did when we first met."

I'm smiling as I say, "I couldn't stand you when we first met. I thought you were cold and unfeeling and arrogant and incredibly obnoxious."

He laughs. "And I thought you were the most stubborn, difficult woman I'd ever met."

For some reason, I like this idea. I like that I made such an impression on him—even if it wasn't an entirely positive one.

We smile at each other for a minute, and it feels like we're sharing something in the gaze, like we're bonding in a way that shouldn't happen through nothing more than a few moments' look.

Soon, I feel a tremor of anxiety and drop the gaze. I need to be careful here. I'm not young anymore. I have absolutely no excuse for being foolish over a man.

Ever again.

To hide the fact that I'm feeling self-conscious, I say in a light voice, "Anyway, back to the point. I like Dr. Martin, and I really think he might be interested in Charlotte."

Dave chuckles and leans back against the bench, his eyes on my face with what looks like affection. "You're not trying to be a matchmaker, are you?"

"Of course not."

"Are you sure?"

"Yes, I'm sure. It's just an instinct I have. The two of them should be together."

"Well, people usually don't end up with the people they should be with, do they?"

I think about that for a moment before I answer. "No. I guess a lot of the time they don't."

We stay at the bench for a little longer than usual, since both of us seem to have lost track of the time. On the walk back, I'm feeling a fluttery excitement that's impossible not to recognize.

I haven't felt this way in a really long time. I didn't think I'd ever feel this way again.

And it worries me anew that I'm feeling it. Dave and I still share only a private, secret walk in the morning. Nothing about his behavior toward me has indicated that he wants to move beyond that.

It's not wrong for me to enjoy the time we have, but I'm not—I'm absolutely not—going to assume it means more than it does.

In its own way, Dave's behavior toward me might be rather like Kevin's to Charlotte—taking advantage of a few secret moments they might spend together but not caring enough to make it public, make it real, make any sort of a commitment.

I glance over at Dave and notice that his eyes are on the path at our feet. This is unusual, as is the slight stiffness of his shoulders.

I wonder if something is hurting him—maybe his arm again, since he kept straining it playing tennis.

We're about to reach the garden when he stops.

I stop too, since it would be weird for me to just keep walking. "Are you okay?" I ask.

"Yes. I'm fine." He's frowning and I don't know why.

"Is your arm bothering you again?"

"No. I just said I was fine."

Now I frown at him. "Well, there's no reason to snap at me."

He gives a rough sigh. "Sorry. But I don't like to be babied."

"I wasn't babying you. I was just asking. It's what polite people do, but you wouldn't know much about that, would you?"

He looks annoyed for a moment, but then he begins to laugh. "I guess you told me."

"I did." I'm trying not to smile now myself.

He clears his throat, looks down again at the path, and then back up to me. "You know, the talk this afternoon is by a regional folklore expert."

"I know," I say, startled by the abrupt change of topic. "I was thinking about going, since it sounds interesting. Usually, those talks seem pretty dumb."

Eagle's Rest brings in someone each Saturday afternoon to give the residents an informative lecture or discussion. Last week it had been fan-making, and the week before the stock market. Neither is of any interest to me, so I hadn't been tempted to attend.

"Yeah. I think so too, but this one might be worth listening to." He clears his throat again. "Would you like to go?"

I stare at him, since we seem to be retreading the same territory in conversation. I just told him I was thinking about going.

But he's looking at me expectantly, and I suddenly realize why. He's asking me to go with him.

With him.

It might just be a walk down the sidewalk to the building next door, but it means something.

The faint fluttering in my chest suddenly picks up intensity.

"Yes," I manage to say, hopefully without looking too startled or fatuous. "That would be fun."

He smiles. He's still a cool customer, even years

past his prime, but I see a faint flicker of what looks like relief at my answer.

That relief makes me ridiculously happy.

"Good," he says with a smile. "I can drop by your place at about two forty-five, if that's okay. That way, we can get good seats."

"Sounds good. I'll be ready."

I say good-bye and turn down the hallway to my apartment.

So maybe I'm smiling like a dope as I unlock my door, but I really don't know how a girl can help it.

eight

There are some disappointments that don't leave you—no matter how many years have passed since they happened.

When I was in high school, Rodney Graham asked me to attend the Christmas formal with him. Rodney was an athlete and very popular with both male and female students. We were lab partners in biology, and so we interacted fairly regularly. He was nice to me. He made me laugh.

I was crazy about him.

When he invited me to attend the dance, I was both shocked and ecstatic. I'd had dates to go to other dances, but they were always with less popular, less attractive boys. My mother and I went shopping for the dress, and we found the most beautiful satin dress—round skirt, fitted bodice, beautiful full sleeves. The dark blue color set off my skin and eyes, and I spent hours on my hair and makeup.

When he picked me up in his Mustang, I felt like a princess. He was friendly and amusing on the drive there, and I'll never forget how everyone watched us as we walked into the school gym together.

All the other girls were envious, unbelieving, that he'd chosen to attend the dance with me. In all my life, I'd never had an experience like that before—the feeling that the best guy had chosen me, that he'd singled me out among all the other girls he could have chosen.

The high lasted for about fifteen minutes—just long enough for us to have one dance and for him to get me a cup of punch. Then his ex-girlfriend showed up, and he started to talk to her. Then he started to dance with her. Then I was completely forgotten.

I left the dance understanding that I'd been put in my place—that kind of Cinderella moment, entering the room like you were really something special, just wasn't intended to happen to me.

For the rest of my life, this truth was confirmed. Not that I've ever considered myself unworthy or unattractive. I've had my share of male attention, and I've had plenty of wonderful moments. It's just that all my highs and lows are well within my expectations for my life.

It's just as well. Time and experience will always confirm that daydreams and fantasies are not the stuff of real life. And when you think for a moment they might be, the real world will come crashing down on you hard, like it did for me at that dance.

All this to say that I have no flights of fancy surrounding my attendance at the afternoon's talk with Dave. I'm happy about it—how could I not be?—but at age seventy-one, I well know what to expect from the world, and this outing doesn't mean more than it actually is.

I do take a little longer than I normally would to decide what to wear, although I end up in one of my usual outfits—a flowing cotton skirt and a blue top that matches my eyes, complete with cardigan and beads. I put lipstick on, but no other makeup, and I decide I look appropriate for an afternoon's activity, while still looking as attractive as is possible for me to be.

I comb my hair down around my shoulders and decide to leave it that way.

At exactly two forty-five, there's a knock on the door, and I walk over to open it. Dave is standing there in the doorway. He's obviously changed clothes since this morning—into a new golf shirt and another pair of trousers—and that fact makes me feel really good.

My heart is fluttering, just a little, but I'm satisfied that my expectations aren't unrealistic or too high.

It's just nice—that he asked me to go with him, that he seems to be taking it seriously, that he's willing to be my companion in public and not just in the privacy of the morning at the bench.

"Are you ready?" he asks, his eyes scanning up and down my body quickly before resting on my face.

"I am. Let me just grab my bag."

I walk to the table to pick up my crocheted purse

and my keys without the walker, which is waiting at the door.

"You don't really need this thing anymore, do you?" he says, glancing down at the walker.

"Not really. I think I would be just fine with my cane." I used a cane on longer walks before the accident, since it helped on the few times I lost my footing. My old cane—of pretty, polished mahogany—is resting near the door, where it always is, as inspiration to keep working at walking so I can get rid of the walker soon.

"Then why don't you switch over to it?" His question is obviously serious, based on genuine curiosity.

"I don't know," I admit. "I kept telling myself I would wait to ask the doctor."

"Did he say you need to get his permission first?"

"No. For driving, but not for using the cane."

He smiles at me, almost whimsically, and reaches over to pick up the cane. "Then why not try it today? We only have a very short walk."

I reach out to accept it but hesitate, a little shiver of nerves surprising me. I have no idea where they've come from.

Dave must see something of my reluctance because he pulls back the cane. "If you're not comfortable, then you can always wait."

I take a shaky breath and reach out for the cane. "I don't know what my problem is. I'll try it. I've been wanting to start using it, and there's no reason to not start today. I just feel . . ."

"What?"

"Insecure or something." I look down at the floor, since that's not something I admit very often—certainly not to other people and usually not even to myself. I've always been independent, resistant to admitting weakness, as far back as that afternoon I almost fell out of the oak tree.

There's no reason for me to say something like that to Dave right now. I really don't know what came over me.

"What's the worst that can happen?" he asks more quietly, as if he's picked up on my state of mind.

I laugh and pull myself out of my introspection. "I could fall down and break another hip."

"I won't let you fall," he murmurs, offering me his arm. His smile seems private, special—and it does something very silly to my heart.

Irony has always been as close to my heart as anything else, so I can't help but tease, "You say that now, but I could take down both of us, I'm sure."

He laughs in response.

I wrap my hand around the arm he's offered, and I use the cane in the other hand as I walk. As we start down the hall, I realize my nerves were unfounded. I've been walking quite well for the last week, and the cane is more than enough to stabilize me as we walk to the side entrance of the building and across the short path to the building next door, where the community rooms are located.

Dave's arm offers me something else.

My expectations are completely realistic. I'm anticipating nothing more than a pleasant afternoon that could very well go no further. So I'm surprised when I walk into the large community room on Dave's arm and see the reaction.

We are early, but nearly all the residents of Eagle's Rest get to activities early. Some folks arrive for lunch at ten thirty. So the room is about half full when we arrive, and everyone is looking at us.

There's a rustle of reaction. I'm not sure why I didn't expect it. Obviously, my showing up with Dave to any sort of function will be a cause for gossip in a place like this. We gossip about everything, since there is not always much else to think about, and there has been considerable interest about Dave's romantic choice for a while now—even a pool going about whether he'll choose Kathy or Gladys.

Both of them are already in attendance—positioned, as usual, at opposite sides of the room. And both of them are shocked and then almost immediately infuriated by the sight of the object of their affection with me.

So they're shooting me down with their eyes as others look on with interest, amusement, surprise, or a mingling of all three. I even see a few female faces look just a little bit envious.

Of me. Of *me*.

If I were still a teenager, my head would have blown this arrival out of all proportion with visions of being Cinderella at the ball. I'm not a teenager, though. I'm not even close. So while I feel a faint fluttering of pleasure, it's tempered with some amusement (at myself, as much as at everyone else) and the sounding bell of wisdom.

After all, the only thing happening here is my walking into a room next to Dave.

Dave appears oblivious to the attention. He's scanning the room, frowning. I'm sure it's because so many people are already here and have claimed the best seats.

"Where do you want to sit?" he murmurs, turning his head to look at me.

I spot a row with the aisle seats empty—the only ones empty on this side of the room. They're midway back, but it won't be any trouble seeing the lectern, and I prefer to be on the side of the room with the door in case I need to get up to use the restroom. "What about there?" I ask, indicating the empty seats.

He nods and leads us over to them.

I feel more comfortable once we're seated. A lot of women would revel in this sort of attention, but I like the idea of it more than the reality. I might have dreamed of being the princess at the ball when I was younger, but I actually prefer for people not to be looking at me all the time.

Dave is still frowning—he's clearly quite annoyed at the seating situation. He gets crabby easily. I've noticed that about a lot of older men—like their filters to life's annoyances have weakened as the years passed. It sometimes makes them seem spoiled or slightly childish.

I don't want him to be grumpy, since it's likely to make me grumpy too. Plus, it's such a little thing that it's not worth worrying about. So I smile up at him. "This is perfect. I like to be close to the door. Thanks for getting these seats."

He smiles in return, relaxing and adjusting his chair slightly, so it's not farther back than the rest of the row. "Good. That worked out well then."

Men—even good, intelligent, strong-willed men— can be led around by their egos.

Marjorie enters the room just now, looking frail but much better than she did yesterday. I wave to her and gesture to the empty seat beside me. She comes over to sit down, and I ask her how she's feeling.

"Oh, much better. Much, much better." She shifts her gaze to Dave. "I was under the weather yesterday."

"I heard you were. I'm glad you're back on your feet." He smiles at her very kindly. "You look wonderful today."

I've got to admit that there's a lot I like about

Dave Andrews. There's a lot I admire about him. And there's a lot about him that I've enjoyed.

But nothing has made me as happy as seeing him smile and speak to Marjorie that way—like she's important, special, worthy of attention—and seeing how much it means to her.

I'm willing to overlook a lot of crabbiness in a man who is kind-hearted enough to do that.

The next morning, I wake up almost an hour early, thinking about Dave.

Yesterday was lovely. We listened to a very interesting talk about folklore in the region. Then Dave, Marjorie, and I went to have tea out on the veranda. At dinner, Dave even came over to sit with Gordon and me instead of heading to one of his normal tables with Gladys or Kathy.

I actually feel a little sorry for those two ladies. They both had such high hopes, and they both worked so hard to snare the man they wanted. It must sting like fire for someone else to come in out of nowhere and swoop him up, right out of their clasp.

Not that I've swooped Dave anywhere. I'm not silly enough to assume that one day means anything. But I'm more excited than I was the day before yesterday—there's potential I didn't believe was possible on Friday—so my mind is whirling with it on Sunday morning, as I look out at the dark gardens and drink my tea.

The sun is rising a little later now than it did when I first arrived. It's already the second half of September. Some of the leaves on the trees in the woods are starting to turn brown.

A few are even falling off the branches.

When it's finally time to dress and leave for the walk, I put on a pair of pants, since it's feeling rather chilly outside, and I take my cane instead of my walker.

I did just fine yesterday. I think I'm finally rid of the walker.

I'm a few minutes too early, and Dave isn't waiting when I go outside. I feel a sharp drop in my chest—an old, familiar knell of Appalachian gloom, reminding me that bad things happen whenever you get too happy.

Maybe Dave won't come out for the walk this morning. Maybe he's already gotten tired of me.

I tell myself not to be stupid, and I wait two minutes until Dave appears at the back door of the building.

He looks surprised when he sees me waiting. "You're early."

"I know," I say. "I woke up early and got bored of sitting around."

This is mostly true, and it's all the truth he needs to know about my state of mind.

"It's a little nippy this morning," he says. He's wearing a light jacket, and he adjusts it so it's falling smoothly around his hips. "Are you going to be warm enough?"

"Of course. This is a warm sweater."

Frowning, he reaches out to feel my sweater between his fingers and thumb. "I guess it will be okay."

I give him a narrow-eyed look. "I told you it was fine."

"Well, I don't want you to be cold."

I can't help but laugh softly, fondly. "I won't be cold. This is my favorite time of the year. There's nothing like autumn."

"Yeah. Nothing like it. The time when everything dies." His voice is dry, but he's smiling as he begins to walk.

"But it dies in such splendor. Even the air feels fresher somehow, like it's putting on its best clothes for the fall of the leaves."

"It's probably because the humidity lessens."

I wrinkle my nose. "You don't have to ruin my poetic thoughts with prosaic science."

He just laughs, and I really like the sound of it.

After a minute, I ask him, "Don't you like the fall?"

"I do. Especially here in the mountains. But I don't think I like it as much as you do."

"I've always loved it." I sniff at the air. "Can't you smell it?"

He sniffs too. "Dirt?"

"No," I reply, giving him an indignant look. "Not just dirt. That's the smell of the fall. You can't smell it any other time of the year."

He laughs again and looks around. It's already light, but the sun is making its first appearance over the mountains in the distance, streaming faint rays out over the valley. "It is a really nice morning."

"I can't understand why so many people just sleep through mornings like this. Evenings are never nearly so nice."

"Evenings have their own appeal, I guess."

For some reason, his words change the mood between us, and I'm not exactly sure why. It's like he's thinking of something else, and his thoughts were somehow evoked through the tone of his voice, although I certainly hadn't heard anything obvious.

But I feel inexplicably excited—in a different way than my pleasure over the fall morning.

We're quiet until we reach the bench, and then I lower myself to sit down, propping the cane against the side. "Now you just sit here and look at that valley and feel the air and tell me you don't think the autumn is the best time of the whole year."

"Do I have to?"

He's mostly teasing, so I give him a look of exaggerated bossiness. "Yes. Sit there and be quiet and learn to appreciate it."

He smiles at me, warm and soft, but then he turns to look out onto the valley. I see him breathing in the air, and I hope he's appreciating it like I do.

I want him to. I want to share it with him.

"It's kind of a rich smell," he says at last, proving he's actually taken my instructions seriously. "Earthy and . . . I don't know . . . full. Like the earth is throwing out everything all at once, because it knows it's nearing the end."

The words touch me, and not just because they prove he's listening to me, caring about what I care about. "Yes. That's it exactly. Spring is lovely, but it's too new to hold nearly so much."

He nods, smiling again but in a different way.

"What are you smiling at?" I ask, since it seems like he has something to say but isn't saying it.

"Nothing. Just you."

I'm starting to feel self-conscious, and I have to fight not to drop my eyes. "What about me?"

"I'm not surprised you like the autumn so much, since you've always been kind of like it."

Now I'm more than self-conscious. I feel a wave of pleasure and intimate connection. I hide it, since that's what I always do. "Oh, you mean old and dirty and nearing the end."

He gives me that frown that's becoming familiar.

"No. I mean how you've always seemed to have more going on inside than you show to the world, like there's so much there that's rich and full that's just beyond the surface. It makes a man want to dig deep."

I don't think anyone has ever said something so nice to me in my entire life. I smile at him, feeling almost shy, which isn't a normal feeling for me anymore. But I'm too experienced to be swept away by the notion, since his words haven't played out as true in my life. "That's a really nice thought, and I appreciate your saying it. But I haven't actually seen it happen."

"Seen what happen?"

"Men wanting to dig deep." I shake my head. "I've never been the belle of the ball."

He's not smiling anymore, and he's looking at me soberly, as if he's thinking through the merits of my words. "I can see that."

"Thanks a lot."

He chuckles. "I just mean that it takes more than a quick glance to see it. Back when we knew each other before, I could never understand why you annoyed me so much, and I think I've finally figured out it's because you scared me."

So I've been liking this conversation up until now, but this isn't what I want to hear. "I wasn't that scary, surely."

"You weren't scary, no. I was just scared because I sensed you might be too much for me."

"You didn't think about me that much back then."

"Not consciously, no. It was just a feeling I had. And I didn't like feeling intimidated—I was used to being able to tackle anything—so it got channeled into annoyance."

"I thought it was just because I was always arguing with you."

"That too."

We smile at each other for a long time, and I feel an entirely new sense of complete understanding, like we've really gotten to know each other, like we're closer than I've been with anyone in a really long time.

If I'm honest, maybe ever.

We sit without talking for several minutes, both of us silently agreeing to let the conversation wash over us, let the morning sink in. After a while, he reaches over to take my hand, the way he did the other day, but today it feels less like comforting.

It feels more like he just wants to touch me, the way I want to touch him.

"Eleanor," he murmurs.

For some reason, the sound of his saying my name both startles and pleases me. People don't actually use my name very much, and when they do it's always Ellie. Hearing him say it feels intimate in a way I really like.

"Yes?" I've been staring out at the valley, but now I turn to him.

"I would like to spend time with you, if that's all right with you."

I blink, that fluttering excitement I've been feeling for the last two weeks intensifying and taking definite shape in my chest. But I'm suddenly nervous, so I do the thing I always do—stall to give myself time to think. "We have been spending time with each other, haven't we?"

"Yes." His eyes are resting on my face quite seriously. "I meant more seriously. If you'd like, of course."

So that's very clear. There's no way I can have misunderstood it or made more of it than it is. He's asking directly, in a very old-fashioned and gentlemanly way that I approve. "I would like that," I manage to say. "I would like that a lot."

He smiles, looking relieved for just a moment the way he did yesterday before he asked me to go to the afternoon talk with him. "Good. I'm glad."

"Me too."

It seems, no matter how many years you live, you still have the potential for very silly conversation.

He reaches over then and lightly strokes my face with his fingers. It's the lightest of touches, but it's shocking somehow—it's been so long since anyone has touched me like that. My skin isn't smooth anymore, but he doesn't seem to care. His eyes are almost hungry. I'd forgotten a man can look that way.

He leans forward slightly. "May I?"

It takes me a moment before I realize he's asking to kiss me. I'm caught up in the same kind of emotional flurry I remember from when I was younger—a blur of excitement that can hardly believe this is happening. "Yes," I whisper.

He goes slowly, scooting over slightly so he doesn't have to lean as much. Then he tilts my head up and his head down until our mouths are a breath apart. I can't really do anything to help him. It's like I'm in a daze.

Then his lips are gently pressing against mine, and it feels just as lovely as I remember, the way kisses always feel when you really want them, when you deeply want to be close to a man. He applies light pressure and pulls away, and then kisses me again, a bit longer this time.

My hand reaches up automatically to rest on his shoulder.

The kiss isn't deep or insistent or overwhelming—it's just full of feeling that leaves me breathless. He pulls away, briefly resting his forehead against mine before he presses one more soft kiss on my mouth and pulls away.

He's smiling when he straightens up, and I imagine I'm smiling too.

But the truth is that it's a full minute before I can think clearly at all.

The next day, Beth takes me out for what she calls a "spa day." What it is, really, is two hours of facials, manicures, and getting our hair done.

Whatever it's called, it's very kind of her to invite me, and I greatly enjoy it.

Beth isn't as bookish or introspective as I am. She's more like her grandmother—my sister—outgoing and friendly, with a warm heart for everyone.

She tells me about the men she's gone out with lately. There are evidently far more of them than I went out with in my entire twenties and thirties. But she's obviously not leading them on. She has fun with them, and I imagine they have fun with her.

Surely one or more of them has fallen in love with her, but it's quite clear to me that she's not fallen in love with any of them.

While we're sitting side by side, getting our nails done, she brings up the topic of Eagle's Rest.

"Is it okay?" she asks, her eyes serious and resting on my face. "Do you think you can be happy there?"

I think of Marjorie and Charlotte and Gordon and the walk that skirts the woods and the bench that looks out on Valentine Valley. I think of people-watching during meals and mornings with my tea on the patio.

I think of Dave.

"Yes," I say. "I really think it's a good place for me. I'm happy."

She lets out an exhale of relief. "I'm so glad. Dad

and I were a little worried, you know. You've always been so independent. And not having your house or a dog or anything, I was afraid . . ." She trails off.

"It is an adjustment," I say softly. I want to tell her the truth and make her feel better. "But I'm adjusting. And there's a lot that I like about Eagle's Rest."

"Good. That's so good. I thought you were looking happier." She gives me a playful look. "Maybe you'll even find a boyfriend."

I have no idea what to say to that. Should I tell her? Is a boyfriend what Dave is to me now?

"What's the matter, Aunt Ellie? I was just teasing. You might find a boyfriend, you know, but I'm sure you'll be plenty happy without one."

"Oh, I know. I knew you were teasing. The truth is there is a gentleman that I've started spending time with."

She looks almost awed—like I told her the best sort of news.

This is a strange thing that happens to people who have been long single. Even if they're happy and successful, everyone acts like the world has finally turned in their favor if they at long last find someone to pair up with.

I don't know why it's always like that, but it is.

"Are you serious?" she asks in almost a whisper.

"Yes. I am. His name is Dave, and he's very nice."

I'm not sure nice is really the best word to describe him, but what else can I say?

"Oh, I'm so excited for you! Are you just starting to date, or is it serious?"

"I don't know how serious it is, but we had a conversation yesterday and we agreed to start spending time together." I use the same words he used, since they're easy and innocuous.

And they're true. We are going to spend time together. And if we also kiss from time to time, then no one else needs to know that right now.

"That's wonderful! Maybe I can meet him sometime." Beth is smiling in her sincere, full-faced way that's so pretty and vibrant.

She's just like her grandmother.

I still miss her grandmother—a lot.

"I'm sure you'll be able to meet him sometime. Maybe you can drop by for tea one day. Something easy and casual."

"Yes, that's perfect. This is the best news ever. Wait until I tell Dad. Aunt Ellie is spending time with someone!"

I've had great joy in my life. I've had great successes. I've had loves and losses and deep feeling. I've had a full, rich life.

But there's still something in the world that believes—that will always believe—that I've never really lived until I get a husband.

I used to believe it too—on nights when I'd be lonely in bed, thinking over all of my failures with men.

I don't believe it anymore. Sometimes wisdom catches up to you. But I decide it's still okay for Beth to be so happy for me.

After all, having found someone to spend time with is a very nice thing indeed.

nine

*F*or the next three weeks, Dave Andrews and I spend time together.

A lot of time together.

We walk together in the mornings, eat our meals together, attend a variety of activities together in the afternoons. I still spend most of the mornings after breakfast in my room, since I get too drained if I'm always around other people, but I spend more time with Dave than I have with anyone since Jeff, who I lived with.

The staff and residents of Eagle's Rest clearly understand that we're a couple. People ask me about Dave now if he's not with me. And even Kathy and Gladys seem to have given up in their obvious pursuit.

I guess it doesn't take long—for something so drastic to change, for someone to transform from a single woman to one half of a couple.

A lot of the time, I still don't believe it, and part of me is just waiting for it to end.

On a Friday morning, he's holding my hand as we reach our bench, and after we sit down, he lifts my hand to his lips and presses a kiss against the knuckles.

He does little things like that a lot. He's by nature

touchier than I am. Not that I'm complaining. I very much enjoy when he kisses me or puts his arm around me, but my natural inclination isn't always to touch the person I'm with, no matter how much I care about him.

Dave is different. Dave likes to touch.

I smile at him and let him pull me against his side so he can put his arm around my shoulders. I lean against him, gazing out at the clouds hanging around the tops of the mountains in the distance.

It's October now. No question about it being fall. The breeze is so crisp it almost bites.

Dave worries when it's cool in the morning, and I know he's going to worry even more when it gets to be winter and I still want to walk—but we'll tackle that issue when it comes up.

After we've been lost in our own thoughts for a while, I ask, "Did Clara ever come up here? Is that why you dedicated the bench to her?"

He shakes his head. "No. She never did. Eagle's Rest was being built when she died, and they were hitting me up for a donation, so I dedicated this bench. I walked around the property and found the most beautiful spot, and I wanted it to always be a gift to Clara."

"That's beautiful. It's a lovely memorial for her. Is that why you came to live here?"

"Yes. I was familiar with the area, of course, but it's mostly because of this bench. It feels like I'm a little closer to her here, and I wanted that for my retirement."

"You could have built a big house and hired a private nurse if you needed one, couldn't you?"

"Yes. I could have done that." His voice is low and unreadable.

"So why didn't you?"

He shrugs slightly. "It would have been lonely."

This rings true to me. Dave has always been more social than me, and I can see why he would want to live somewhere that would offer him a real community, especially since relations with his stepfamily seem a little strained.

We let the subject drop, and I wonder if he's still thinking about it like I am.

"Do you still want to go to the craft fair tomorrow?" he asks after a few minutes of silence. We still don't have to talk all the time, and that's one of the best things about him, as far as I'm concerned.

"Yes. I'm looking forward to it."

There's a large craft fair every year in the nearby college town, and I've gone every year for decades. I'm excited about going again this year, and I'm pleased that Dave wants to go with me.

"Kevin called this afternoon," Dave says, a different note in his voice. "He was wondering if we want to have lunch with him tomorrow, since we'll be in town in the morning for the fair."

I pull away from him just enough to look up in his

face and see he's slightly reluctant, like he doesn't know what I'll think about this idea. "That would be okay, I guess. He wants to have lunch with me too?"

"Yes. He said he'd like to get to know you, since we're . . ."

"We're what?" I ask, with a teasing smile.

"We're together."

My smile widens. "Is that what we are?"

Smiling in response, he leans over and kisses me softly on the lips. "Yes. Together is what we are."

It's so unexpected—to feel this way at my age, to have fallen for a man like this so late in my life, right when I was thinking that everything important was over. I'm still not sure how it's even happened.

And I'm also not sure how long it can possibly last.

"I'd be happy to have lunch with him," I say, speaking the truth. I'd like to get to know Dave's stepson a little more, to find out if what I suspect is based in reality. "Will it just be him?"

"Probably not. His brother and sisters are in town. They live in Virginia Beach, you know, but they've come for a visit."

"Oh my. It will be a big group."

"Is that okay?" He looks at my face closely.

"Yes, it's okay. I can't promise to be charming, though."

He laughs. "I never would have expected you to be."

"Is that right?"

He tightens his arm around me briefly in a kind of half hug. "I know you don't like big groups. You can sit there without talking as far as I'm concerned. It's mostly just going through the motions."

"You don't like them? Your stepchildren, I mean?"

He gives a slight shrug I feel rather than see. "They are what they are. Obviously, I didn't choose them, but I'm not going to abandon them now. They're the only family I have."

"Yes. Of course they are." I feel bad for asking about it, since now he sounds rather glum. To change the subject, I add, "The van is scheduled to return here at noon tomorrow." Eagle's Rest is providing transportation for the residents who want to attend the craft fair, and we were planning to use the van since that's the easiest way to get around. "We'll have to change our plans."

"I'm sure Kevin or one of the others will bring us back," Dave says. He sighs. "I wish I could drive, but they still won't let me."

"They" in this context is the DMV, not his stepchildren. He told me last week that he has had a couple of episodes where he lost consciousness—one of them while he was driving. Legally, this means he can't drive for a certain number of months. The incidents were evidently some neurological quirk, and they're also the reason he moved from the independent-living cottage to the assisted-living building.

It worries me—that something is wrong with him that they can't quite identify. But he's otherwise quite healthy, so I try not to brood about it.

At our age, everyone has some kind of health issue.

"I can drive," I say, thinking of my car, which has been parked in the lot here but rarely used since I arrived. "That might be easier. We don't have to take the van at all, and I can just drive us there and back."

I can tell Dave is frowning, even though I'm not looking at his face because he's still holding me against his side. "You don't have to."

I pull away, straightening up. "You're not going to get all weird about it being me driving and not you, are you?"

"Of course not."

"Then why are you all tense and bristly?"

He narrows his eyes. "I'm not."

"Yes, you are. You think I can't tell? What's the problem about me driving?"

He sighs, evidently giving up on his resistance. "There's no problem. It will be more convenient that way, so of course you can. It's just that, in my day, the man did the driving."

I smile at him, feeling fond. "Your day is my day too, you know. It's just that I've changed with the times."

"And I haven't?"

I reach out to stroke the side of his face, my fingers

stroking back to his thinning hair. "Not in this, it seems like. I promise I won't bring you flowers or open doors for you. How's that?"

He chuckles, his hand going up to cover mine on his face. "I can live with that."

Our plans for tomorrow are decided, and we relax back on the bench to enjoy a few more minutes of the morning before it's time to return for breakfast.

I'm glad he's okay with my driving. I think it's the right, most reasonable thing for him to do. But as I sit and think, I start to realize that he just gave up on his resistance, the way he often does.

He told me straight out, not so long ago, that it's not worth the effort to fight anymore.

I don't like that idea.

Obviously, I don't think one needs to fight over trivial issues or wrong-headed notions. But surely some things are worth fighting over. I wonder if Dave would be willing to fight for anything.

I wonder if he would be willing to fight for me.

The next day, I drive Dave into town—the same town where both of us once worked at the college. I know of a good parking lot that's not known to a lot of the public, so we're able to get a good parking spot that doesn't require much walking.

The craft booths are all set up along a few main streets in town, which are closed down for the weekend to accommodate the fair.

Saturday morning is the best time to go, since it doesn't get really crowded until the afternoon. So Dave and I have a good time strolling around, stopping to look at unique items, talk to the craftspeople, and get snacks like roasted oranges and funnel cakes.

I enjoy myself, and Dave buys me three different strings of beads I admire and an adorable bouquet of wooden flowers. He would buy me more if I'd let him, but I don't want to take advantage of his generosity.

He seems to be enjoying himself too, and I grow aware of people watching us occasionally.

This is what I've been discovering lately. If an older person is by herself, she often becomes invisible —just part of the background. But, if she's part of a couple, they suddenly become "cute."

When Dave holds my hand as we walk, I see a variety of people looking in our direction and smiling, as if there's something particularly adorable about such an innocent and commonplace gesture. And when he leans over to kiss me as I'm gushing over a collection of lovely crocheted purses, the woman who made them makes this expression that speaks as loud as words, saying, *Aw, how sweet.*

It bothers me a little, even though I know all these people are well-intentioned and good-hearted. There's something patronizing about these responses, as if normal human interaction somehow becomes something to be sighed over, like a kitten or a child.

Just because we're older.

It makes me feel vulnerable in that way I've never liked to feel.

I make myself push the idea out of my mind. After all, it doesn't matter what anyone else thinks about me—or about Dave. Pretty soon, we'll return to Eagle's Rest, where being older is the norm and no one looks at us strangely.

"Did you want one of those purses?" Dave asks, as we walk away.

"Oh, no. They're lovely, but that's the last thing I need."

"If you like them, I'll buy you one." He starts to turn around as if he's about to go back.

"No, no." I hold onto his arm so he can't leave. "I don't want you to buy me everything I happen to like."

He gives me a curious look. "Why not? I like to buy you things."

I can tell that's true. He's a man who's had a lot of money for most of his life, and he's probably gotten into the habit of buying things to express his affection.

But I've been a woman who has always been self-sufficient, and I don't like to accept a lot of gifts. They make me feel obligated, something I've never been comfortable with.

Instead of telling him all this, I just say, "I don't

have room for a lot of stuff anymore. I love the beads and flowers you already bought me."

He smiles, evidently satisfied with this response. "Do you want to rest for a few minutes before we walk back to the car? There's an empty bench there."

I nod. We've been on our feet longer this morning than we normally are, and I at least am feeling it in my legs, back, and the hip that wasn't replaced.

My new hip doesn't hurt at all.

We have lunch at a French restaurant that's opened just recently in town. The location is central, so we don't have to repark the car, but the seating is cramped, the atmosphere is pretentious, and the menu is far too expensive for a small college town like this.

I wish they'd chosen somewhere else for us to have lunch.

I don't complain, though. I'm just along for the ride, and I don't want to make Dave feel bad. My impression of his stepchildren doesn't improve from their choice of restaurant, however.

I try to keep a good attitude. I shouldn't be so judgmental. My first impressions aren't always accurate, after all.

They usually are.

I sit next to Dave, with my back up against a wall

in a way that doesn't allow me to stretch my hip. This isn't exactly comfortable, but Dave keeps looking over at me, as if to check to make sure I'm all right, so I maintain a pleasant smile, even when I just want to escape to my room and close the door on the rest of the world.

The whole crew is here. Kevin. His brother, Rick, and his girlfriend, Maylene. His two sisters, Jenny and Tiffany. And Tiffany's husband, Howie.

Jenny and Tiffany are both well-dressed and overly nice, so much so that it feels fake to me. Rick doesn't talk much, except to Maylene, and Kevin clearly sees himself as the ringleader of this circus.

The service at the restaurant is very slow, so I'm ravenous after we've been seated for forty minutes and the food still hasn't come. The bread is too dry for my taste, and they give only a small, hard pat of butter to go with it. I keep trying to eat pinches of it, but I hate dry bread without butter.

"We were so thrilled when we heard Papa Dave had found himself a lady friend," Tiffany is saying. She's the kind of woman who fights off any sign of aging with all her might. I'm pretty sure she's had cosmetic surgery already, although she's just in her early forties.

Papa Dave. A very annoying appellation, and one they evidently all used.

I smile, since I'm supposed to, but what kind of answer am I supposed to give to such a statement?

"You're a dark horse, aren't you, old man?" Kevin says, elbowing Dave. "Who would have thought?"

Dave arches his eyebrows. "We're not dead yet, you know."

"I'm just glad you didn't get taken advantage of by some chick forty years younger than you." That's Tiffany again.

Dave could find himself a much younger girlfriend. Quite easily, I'm sure. He's in fairly good health for his age and is still attractive, maybe even to a woman younger than I am. He also has money, which is often the deciding factor.

Sometimes I wonder why he hasn't looked for a younger girlfriend like so many men in his position do. Then I tell myself to stop wondering, since that line of thought is fruitless.

"Of course you're not dead," Kevin says, pounding on Dave's back the way men sometimes do. Dave winces slightly, as if he doesn't appreciate the pounding. "You're doing great for your age."

"And what's this I hear about you winning the community tennis match?" Tiffany again.

I have no idea what she's talking about. Dave hasn't won a tennis match since I've been living at Eagle's Rest.

"That was three months ago," Dave says, with another lift of his eyebrows.

And on and on it goes, in much the same fashion. They talk to him like he's deaf and a little soft in the head, like a puppy who has performed unexpect-edly well.

I shouldn't be so harsh with them. They're not acting all that different from the way a lot of people interact with those our age. But still . . . they drive me crazy, and I'm hard-pressed to keep listening to it without rolling my eyes and making faces.

At one point, Dave looks over at me while I'm pinching off another bite of bread, hoping to stave off my starvation.

Without saying anything, he takes his knife and moves his pat of butter, which he's left mostly un-touched, over to my plate.

I smile at him, since this is very sweet and much appreciated.

I glance up and catch a surprisingly calculat-ing look from Jenny. I don't know for sure what she's thinking, but I can make a pretty good guess. She thinks I'm making a play for Dave and might threaten her inheritance.

They probably all feel the same way. They don't want Dave to hook up with anyone. They want to ensure they're the only ones he'll be leaving his money to.

I don't want Dave's money, and I'm quite sure he knows that. There's no reason to think he'll die before me anyway. He's only a few years older than me, after all.

The food finally arrives, and, while it's lukewarm

and rather strange, at least it's edible. It also gives everyone something other to do than make annoying comments at Dave.

The second half of lunch is dominated by Tiffany and Jenny's plans for a Caribbean spa vacation and Kevin's complaints about how his car has so many problems he needs a new one.

Neither of these topics is of interest to me. Both of the topics seem to lead toward a variety of hints for Dave to help out in a monetary fashion.

At one point, I'm so exasperated, I'm on the verge of saying that, in my day, we didn't take vacations or buy cars we couldn't afford. That's not entirely true, but it's certainly truer than it is of people now.

But I glance over at Dave and see that he's looking rather stretched, like he's ready for the lunch to end, and I bite my tongue.

I don't want to make things awkward for Dave by getting on the wrong side of his stepchildren. I'm probably already on the wrong side, simply by virtue of the fact that I'm dating him, but there's no sense in making it worse.

Some people, as they age, have fewer and fewer inhibitions about the things that come out of their mouths. I'm the opposite. As I've gotten older, I've found myself thinking through my words more carefully.

The pleasure one feels at saying what one thinks

can be nice. But it's rarely worth the negative consequences.

The lunch finally ends, and they all line up to give Dave hugs or kisses. They try to kiss me too, but I stick my hand out at them instead, so they shake my hand, one after the other, like an awkward receiving line at a wedding.

"Do you need any help getting home?" Kevin asks, as we're leaving the restaurant.

"No." Dave has gotten curter as the lunch has gone on, and he's now in that grumpy state where he just grunts out responses.

He's been like that with me several times, but today I find the attitude completely understandable.

"Are you sure?" Tiffany asks. I notice that her makeup has little cracks around the eyes, and I find this detail unreasonably unattractive. "We'll be happy to make sure you get back safely."

"No," Dave says again.

"I drove my car," I say, trying to smooth over this interaction so we can get the heck out of here. "We'll be fine."

"Oh, wonderful! How nice that you still drive!"

I manage not to roll my eyes at Tiffany, and then we're finally, finally out of the building and parting ways with the others.

I take Dave's arm as we walk to the car and don't say anything. He's obviously not in the mood to talk, so I just let him know I'm here—in the hope that my presence might help him feel better.

He doesn't talk on the way to the car, and he doesn't talk on the drive back up to Eagle's Rest. In fact, we're getting out of the car and starting back to our building before he finally responds in any way.

He reaches over and pulls me toward him, pressing a soft kiss on my temple.

I look up at his face. "What's that for?"

He gives a tired smile. "That's for putting up with lunch with that pack of wolves."

Evidently, he has the same thoughts about them that I do. It's vaguely comforting, since it means I probably didn't make it up out of my own judgmental spirit.

Believe it or not, that's happened a time or two.

"Maybe they're not really that bad," I say. I put my hand on his side and really like the feel of his solid flesh beneath his shirt. He's not perfectly lean and hard, the way he was in his forties, when I knew him before. (Not that I ever touched him back then, but, still, a woman can tell.) It doesn't matter that he's soft around his middle and a little bony higher up, toward his ribs. I like the feel of it. He feels like a man. And it's nice to touch them sometimes.

"Do you think so?" The irony is obvious in the dryness of his voice.

"Well, if you can tell what they're really like, then why do you put up with them?"

He frowns. "I told you before. They're the only family I have."

"I guess so, but it's a lot to put up with, just to have a family connection." I'm not entirely sure I should be saying this. My pulse has picked up with anxiety, the sign that I might be saying too much.

He gives that shrug I've seen from him a lot of times, the gesture where he's resigning himself to the world. "What other choice do I have?"

"Well, you could just not spend much time with them. You could not let them take advantage of you."

"They don't take advantage of me. I know what they're like." He looks a little offended now, as I've evidently bruised his ego.

He used to be a powerful man, in control of circumstances and the people in his orbit. That's not the case anymore, and it must be hard for him sometimes to come to terms with it.

I probably shouldn't have reminded him.

"I know you do. I'm sure it's all fine." I reach up so my hand is spanning the back of his neck. "It would just be nice if they loved you."

He gives that shrug again and doesn't say anything, but he's holding my gaze, like he understands what I'm trying to express.

Wanting to be encouraging, I add, "Maybe they do, in their own way."

He shakes his head. "Clara loved me."

And that's just heartbreaking—that he had a child

once who loved him the way he needs to be loved, the way he deserves to be loved, and then he lost her.

My face twists as emotion surges up into my throat, and I make a funny little sound as I wrap both of my arms around his neck.

He returns the hug. We hold each other for a long time.

It's easy, at our stage of life, to feel alone—to feel like the rest of the world has simply outrun us. So many people at Eagle's Rest feel lonely so much of the time, and all of the planned activities in the world can't necessarily counteract the feeling.

I don't feel lonely right now, though, my arms around Dave, his holding me very tightly. I don't feel alone.

And I'm absolutely sure that he doesn't feel alone right now either.

ten

I t's two weeks later, on a gray, chilly Sunday, when Marjorie dies.

I go to church in the morning. Dave was kind of grumpy earlier on our walk, and I feel glum, in need of spiritual refreshment.

So I join a small group of residents who attend a nearby Baptist church. We go to the early service and stay for the coffee time afterward, so it's almost eleven before we return to Eagle's Rest. I'm hoping Dave's mood has improved. If it hasn't, I'm going to leave him on his own and watch British mysteries in my apartment all afternoon by myself.

I've always enjoyed afternoons like that, and it's certainly better than trying to entertain an old man in a bad mood.

But as soon as I arrive back home, Charlotte comes to find me. She tells me that I should visit Marjorie, and she looks so sober that I feel a chill of concern.

My anxiety is realized when I enter Marjorie's room. It's very dark, with the blinds closed and the overhead lights off. And there's a feeling in the air that's silent, despairing.

I swallow hard as I walk over to Marjorie's bed. She's lying under the covers, the way she did a few weeks ago when she had the bad episode, and she looks so pale and frail it's like she's almost transparent—like it will just take a few more minutes for her small body to dissolve into nothingness.

I've lived a long time, and I've seen my share of death. I'm not fooled about the situation this time. She's near the end.

"Ellie," she says when she sees me. "I'm so glad you're here."

"Charlotte told me you could use a visit."

"I wanted to see you. I was . . . I was lonely."

Hearing something like that—from a spirit as sweet as Marjorie's—is painful. She should be surrounded by friends and family right now, and all she has is Charlotte and me.

Charlotte looks like she's close to tears when I glance back at her. She says, "I've called Dr. Martin."

I nod and turn back. "I'll stay with you as long as you like."

"Good. I'm tired right now. We can talk later."

"Of course we can. You just rest."

She's told me the name of her exact condition in the past, but I can never remember what it is. It basically boils down to her heart giving out. There may be some treatments she could try to extend her life, but at her age she doesn't want to bother with them.

Maybe it's easier this way, after all. To just fade away. Here, in these rooms that she loves.

In books and movies, deathbed scenes are always

sentimental or dramatic, with all the words that need to be said actually said. It rarely happens that way in real life. Marjorie isn't really in the state to say much of anything. She sleeps until Dr. Martin arrives, and he examines her, shaking his head.

There's clearly nothing to be done that she's willing to have done.

I sit in a chair beside her bed and watch her go.

There's one point when she wakes up and seems to see me, recognize me. She asks faintly, "My dear, do you enjoy knitting?"

It's only then that I tear up.

I'm not much of a crier. I never have been. But it doesn't mean I don't feel things just as deeply as other people.

I tell Marjorie that I've never learned to knit, and she drifts off, away from me again.

It's quite a while before she dies for real, but she seems gone before then. Her breathing gets harsher, more labored, like it's an effort for her to breathe at all. And Charlotte, Dr. Martin, and I all suffer through it with her as she breathes less and less, as she twists in discomfort, as the spark that has always been *Marjorie* goes out.

Finally, Dr. Martin steps over and puts his hand just in front of her mouth and nose. Then he reaches down to feel the pulse in her neck.

"That's it," he says. "Time of death, four thirty-three."

He nods toward the nurse who has come in earlier, so she can record it properly, and I just sit in my chair, unable to move.

I've been here for hours, evidently. Gayle is here now too. She must have come in at some point, maybe with the nurse, although I have no idea when. I vaguely wonder why Dave hasn't come to look for me.

It doesn't really matter, though. Today has been harder on me than anything in a really long time. I'd rather be alone with it.

I don't move until I'm aware of Charlotte, pulling gently on my arm. "You should leave, Ellie," she says. "There's nothing else for you to do here. Let me help you back to your room."

I nod and find myself standing up, walking slowly out of the room and down the hall toward my apartment. It's only halfway there that I realize that Dr. Martin is walking with us, supporting me with an arm.

I haven't even been aware of his presence, just that I seem to be moving.

They get me to my recliner, and Charlotte murmurs she'll make me a cup of tea. Dr. Martin is peering at my face, checking my pulse and responses. I'm not sure what he thinks might be wrong with me, but my body is just fine, aside from sitting in the same position for too long.

Charlotte brings over the cup of tea. "Where is Dave, anyway?" she asks.

"I don't know."

"I'll go look for him. I'm not sure you should be alone."

"I'm fine." I'm convinced the words are true. I'm just sad, as anyone would be.

"I'll find him for you."

"I'd rather be alone."

Charlotte shakes her head and meets Dr. Martin's eyes. His expression is as gentle and understanding as always, and I can tell they've shared a thought without words.

The thought is very likely about me, but there's nothing I can do about it.

All I can do is sit here at the moment.

I sip my tea, and it actually helps, although Charlotte has made it overly sweet. Soon, Dr. Martin leaves, since there must be a lot of logistics to take care of now that Marjorie has died. Charlotte leaves, saying she'll find Dave.

After half a cup of tea, I'm revived enough to check my phone. I see that Dave has called twice. The first time, he didn't leave a message, but the second time he did. He asked if I wanted to go into town with him this afternoon to hear a string quartet concert.

I never replied to his message, so he probably just went without me.

It's just as well. I prefer to sit here on my own.

That doesn't end up happening, though. In a few minutes, Charlotte returns, saying that Dave isn't at the residence but she called him and he's on his way back.

That makes me feel weird, weak, like I'm in need of help, like Dave needs to run to my rescue.

I'm not in need. I'll be fine if I can just sit and be left alone.

But Charlotte fusses around for another half hour, until Dave is knocking on the door. He has clearly hurried back, and he looks urgent and concerned.

He comes over to sit beside me, reaching to take my hand. "Why didn't you tell me?" he asks.

I don't answer that question. It's a foolish question, and I don't have an answer for him anyway.

"I would have stayed with you the whole time," he murmurs, his dark eyes searching my face in that way he has.

I don't want him searching my face at the moment. I don't want him knowing what I'm feeling. I just want to be left alone. "I'm fine," I say, my voice cracking on the last word.

His expression tightens, a detail I'm aware of, but he doesn't argue or insist. He just glances over to meet Charlotte's eyes.

I don't like that. I don't like when people are meeting eyes behind my back, having silent conversations about me. It makes me feel old and helpless.

Charlotte leaves a few minutes later, but Dave stays. He gets me another cup of tea. He tucks a crocheted blanket around my lap and legs. He sits and holds my hand and looks at me.

I know he's trying to help. I know he doesn't know what else to do. But, although I hate to admit it, the truth is he's getting on my nerves.

Finally, I manage to say with something of my normal composure, "Please don't fuss."

"I wasn't saying anything."

"I can feel you fussing silently."

He lets out a long breath. "I'm worried about you."

"I know, but you don't have to be. It was hard watching her die. It always is. I'm sad about it." Saying the words, I feel something start to crack inside me, so I throw up my mental defenses, which are very strong after years of practice. "But I knew it was going to happen soon, and it was probably the right time. I'm not going to fall apart or anything."

"I didn't say you would fall apart. You just seem . . ."

You see, I don't like that either, like he thinks I'm weak, not capable of handling life's challenges.

I've always been capable. I've always been strong. I've always been perfectly able to deal with the ups and downs of life on my own.

That hasn't changed now, just because I'm over seventy and spending time with Dave.

"I'm fine," I say again, a little of my impatience evident in my voice now.

He must hear it. "Okay. Just tell me if there's anything I can do."

"You don't have to stay with me."

"I'm not going to leave."

I hear that it will be useless to argue with him about this. Under normal circumstances, I'm a lot more stubborn than he is—at least now that he's taken that resigned attitude toward life—but I'm not in my normal condition right now, and I can sense he's not going to be moved. So I just say, "Okay. Then I'd like to just be quiet for a while, if that's okay."

He still looks concerned, as if he doesn't believe I really need what I say I need. He doesn't argue, though. We sit for a while in silence until it becomes oppressive, and then we put on a British mystery episode I've seen dozens of times.

The familiarity is comforting, so we watch two more episodes after the first one is over. I can see he keeps wanting to touch me—like he thinks cuddling me will make me feel better—but I know I can't stand that right now. I let him hold my hand for as long as I can handle, but eventually I have to pull even that away.

Fortunately, I stay in my recliner, so it's not like we're sharing the couch.

Charlotte brings us dinner in my room, and he doesn't appear inclined to leave afterward. At seven thirty, I finally have to tell him that I'm tired and just want to shower and go to bed.

He doesn't want to leave me alone, but I feel strong enough to insist on it now, so I finally get him out.

I feel guilty for it afterward, but I'm also relieved.

I just want to be alone. I don't know why people can't understand that. Everyone is different, and not everyone needs to be coddled endlessly when they've gone through something difficult.

I don't like to feel weak, and that's how Dave is making me feel.

I take a shower and get ready for bed, and then I put on another mystery so I can watch it from bed.

I watch three more before I'm finally able to sleep.

I don't wake up until after five thirty the following morning, which is much later than usual for me. I feel groggy and aching and so depressed I can barely get up.

I make myself, since I have no excuse to lie about in bed, and I'm relieved to discover that it's raining steadily outside.

I stare out at the darkness and feel irrationally vindicated, like nature has somehow matched my mood. It also gives me an excuse to skip my morning walk. Otherwise, Dave would be very worried if I said I didn't want to go.

I don't want to go. I don't really want to see him. I just want to spend the day in my room and watch television or read books.

My phone rings, and I reluctantly answer it, since I know it's Dave and he'll be over here knocking on my door if I don't pick it up.

"Good morning," he says.

"Hi."

"How are you feeling?"

"I'm fine."

He hesitates, as if he doesn't believe me, but he doesn't pursue the topic. "I guess there's too much rain for a walk this morning."

"Yeah, I think so."

"Shall I come over there? We can sit and watch the rain." We've done that before, on the occasional rainy morning.

"I was actually thinking I might sleep in," I lied. "If that's okay."

"Of course it's okay." What else can he say, after all? But he sounds strange, kind of tight. "Just let me know when you're up, and I'll come over."

"Okay."

I hang up, relieved, and I make myself another cup of tea. At least I've given myself a respite for the morning.

Dave makes it until ten o'clock before he's knocking on my door.

I was hoping he'd hold out until lunch, but I guess that was wishful thinking.

He's frowning soberly as I open the door, and he scans me from head to toe. I'm obviously up and dressed, since I'm wearing loose pants and a sweatshirt.

"I thought you were going to call me when you got up."

"I was. I mean, I was going to call you. I just wanted a little time to myself."

He doesn't look like he believes me. "The rain has slacked off now. We can go for a walk before lunch, if you want."

I don't want to walk. I don't even want to go to lunch. "I think I'd rather just hang out here." I don't step out of the doorway.

"Am I invited in?" he asks.

I make a face. "There's not much time before lunch anyway. We can see each other this afternoon, if you want."

"It's not about what I want. It's about what's good for you. I'm worried about you."

"I know you are, but I'm obviously not falling apart."

"It doesn't feel that way to me. You're never like this."

I feel a clench of resentment. "Like what?"

"Like you're closing me out."

I can't hold back an exasperated sigh. It sounds almost like a groan. "Dave, please. Yesterday was hard for me."

"I know it was hard. That's why I'm worried. That's why I don't think you should be alone. I don't think this is good for you."

This is all too much. It's one thing to know that he's thinking it. It's another to hear him say it out loud. "That's not fair. Not everyone recovers emotionally in the same way. I need to be alone to . . . to recover. It's not about you."

"I know it's not about me."

This is going on so long that I need to end it immediately. It feels like I'm going to cry, and there's no way I'll do it in front of Dave.

Or in front of anyone.

So I do what I know will work, even if it's unfair and rather underhanded. I say, "Well, it feels like you're making it about you—thinking about what you want instead of what I need. I'm telling you that what I need is a little time, and I think it's a little selfish of you to act like you know better than me about my own needs."

I see the reaction on his face—half guilt, half frustration. There's nothing he can say now. I've left him with no leg to stand on.

So he says, "Okay. But I'm not going to let you hibernate all day. Can we do something this afternoon?"

"Yes," I say, mostly to get him out of here before I crack. "You can come by this afternoon, if you want."

He opens his mouth to reply, but I close the door on him.

I return to my recliner, rubbing my eyes and trying to suppress the shuddering.

This is terrible. Everything was going just fine. Dave and I were getting along so well.

But now we'd finally run up against one of the absolute truths of my life.

I've always been self-sufficient, and that's never going to change. I have to get through the hardest things alone.

And I somehow know that Dave isn't going to accept that.

Which means he's probably going to end up leaving me.

That's always how it works for me, so I can hardly be surprised.

Dave is knocking on my door again at one thirty in

the afternoon, and I let him in, since I don't have the energy to put up a fight.

He wants to go out and do something, so I agree to walk in the gardens with him. I don't want to go up the path to the bench, even though he tries to talk me into it.

I don't know why he won't just give me a day or two to be sad on my own. Then I'll be back to normal, and we can return to how things were. But he doesn't seem inclined to leave me. When he walks me back to my apartment, he comes inside with me.

We end up watching more British mysteries until dinner time. Then I make myself go to the dining room with him so he won't worry about me as much.

He keeps watching me, an unspoken question in his eyes. And no matter how normal I try to act, it doesn't seem to ease his worries.

When he wants to sit with me some more in the evening, I'm about to lose my patience. It's not even seven yet when I tell him I'm tired and want to go to bed.

"It's early," he says, looking surprised as he glances at his watch.

"I'm tired."

"You're more than tired."

It's very hard not to snap his head off. "That's why I need to be alone."

"So you keep saying."

"I keep saying it because you never seem to listen."

"I am listening." He rubs a hand over his jaw, like

he's trying to channel some sort of angst in an innocuous way. "I just can't believe that hiding away like this is what you really need."

I actually groan. "Is it not possible that people cope in different ways?"

"Of course it's possible. But you're not talking to me at all. You're pretending that everything is fine, when I know it's not."

"I'm sad," I say, raising my voice because he just won't leave me alone. "I'm sad. I cared about Marjorie, and now she's dead. I watched for hours as she died. How else am I supposed to feel? I'm *sad*. I've told you that. What else do you need to know?"

"I want to know why you feel like you can't *act* sad with me! I want to know why you think leaning on me, even a little, means you're weak."

"I don't think that." It's a lie, though. He's got it exactly right. "You don't understand me at all."

I stand up because ending this conversation is the only thing left available to me now unless I want to break down and sob because I can't hold back the emotions anymore.

This is just too much to deal with on top of Marjorie's death.

"I know you're trying to help, but you don't understand me at all. And I think I'd like you to leave now so I can go to bed."

This should work. After all, the apartment is mine, not his. He has to leave when I tell him to.

He stands up too. "I'm not going to leave until I know that you're okay. And right now, you're not."

"You have to leave. I am okay."

He's shaking his head, his expression tense and determined. "You're not okay. Why are you lying to me?"

"Please, Dave," I say, at the very edge of my control. I'm shaking all over now, but there's no way to stop it. "Please just leave."

He makes a throaty sound and reaches out to pull me into his arms. "I'm not going to leave," he says against my hair. "Not when you need me. I don't know why you think I will."

And that's it. I start to cry.

Once I start, I can't stop, and it's really quite messy and embarrassing. I sob against his chest as he holds me wrapped in his arms.

I never do this. Never. Even with Jeff, I only let him hug me after the worst of it was over.

Dave is saying again, "I'm not going to leave you," and I can tell that he means it.

In spite of everything I know about myself, the words, the touch, the knowledge of who Dave is, make me feel just a little bit better.

eleven

*W*e end up on the couch together.

It's partly because I'm so exhausted I'm not sure I can keep my feet. And it's partly because we don't want to let go of each other.

I know being so touchy isn't usually my thing, but it feels like the right thing at the moment—what both Dave and I need. And it's nice.

I'm not crying anymore. All the emotion has worn itself out. It's really nice now to feel his arm around me, to feel his body against mine, to feel like he's genuinely here for me—all the way, just as I need him to be.

We don't turn on the television this time. We just sit together, listening to the sound of the drizzle outside. I'm stroking his chest and belly with my hand, and both our bodies are relaxed.

He must be able to sense that I'm feeling better, because he loosens his arm from around me and starts to caress my hair. Then he murmurs, "Why was that so hard for you?"

"I don't know. I'm just not used to . . . I'm used to dealing with things on my own."

"But you don't have to now."

"I know." I swallow hard because I'm starting to

feel guilty, like I somehow failed him, failed our relationship. "I'm sorry."

"You don't have to be sorry. I just want to know why it was so hard, why you felt like you needed to close me out."

For most of my life, I've avoided conversations like this. They never seemed really necessary, since my relationships usually worked fine without a lot of soul searching. Even with Jeff, we were intimate with our bodies but not with our words.

So I'm uncomfortable with this, but I don't want to disappoint Dave again. "I wasn't trying to shut you out. I've just always handled hard things by myself, so it doesn't feel natural for me to lean on someone or look to someone else for help. I know it's not right—and it's not fair to you—but the habits of a lifetime are hard to break. I've always been alone."

He's still stroking me, and I feel him nodding, as if he understands. Then he tilts his head down to brush a kiss into my hair. "You're not alone anymore."

I look up at him now, because I want to see his face, because I want to see his expression to really understand. His eyes are sober, a little hesitant. "I'm not?" I ask, the slightest bit of crack in my voice.

He leans down to kiss my lips softly. "You're not."

"Okay."

"Good."

He smiles and pulls me into a gentle hug. I hug him back and then relax against him once again.

We stay like that for another half hour, until I'm having to shift every few minutes to get more comfortable. My hip doesn't do this position very easily, and the rest of my body isn't used to it. Either my back hurts or my leg hurts or my hip hurts, however I position my weight. I don't want to pull away from him, but I'm not sure how much longer I can stay like this.

"Do you need to adjust?" he asks, after I shift slightly to keep the weight off my hip.

"I think so. I'm sorry. My joints aren't appreciating the position."

"My shoulder is bothering me too. You look really tired, anyway. Do you want to go to bed?"

I do want to go to bed. I'm so tired I can barely think now, and it's close to my regular bedtime. But I don't want to send Dave away, not after everything that's happened. "I guess so."

He gives one of those uncertain eye shifts from my face to the floor and then back. "Do you want me to stay with you?"

My lips part slightly as I try to process this question.

He adds, "Just to sleep. I'd like to stay with you— I'd like to be close to you—if it's okay with you. I wouldn't be hinting after anything else tonight."

Sometimes I wonder if he thinks about having sex with me, but he's never mentioned it, and I've never brought it up. But never would I have dreamed he'd make some sort of move like that tonight. My hesitance is based on something entirely different. "So you just want to . . . to sleep with me?"

"Would that be okay? I don't want to leave you."

I'm not really comfortable with it. I haven't shared my bed with anyone for almost twenty years, and I never expected to do so again. But I want to be close to Dave, and I want him to know it, so I nod, dropping my eyes. "Okay."

I glance up as practical matters distract me. "Will you be comfortable sleeping in . . . in what you've got on?"

He glances down at himself. "I'll go to my room and change and then come back."

It makes sense, and I agree as I walk with him to the door and watch him start down the hall. There's no one around. I'm relieved. Because now it all feels planned, intentional, not a spontaneous decision based on mutual neediness.

Right now, we're going through logistics to actually bring it about, and the idea of sleeping with Dave —sex or not—makes my heart flutter with anxiety.

There's no sense in brooding about it, though, since it's obviously going to happen. So I use the time wisely and change into a robe and nightgown and wash up for bed.

I'm straightening my bedding when there's a knock on the door. I go to get it quickly, since I don't want anyone to see him waiting at my door.

He's wearing black lounge pants and a T-shirt, and he looks at me closely as I open the door.

"What are you staring at?"

"Just seeing if you've changed your mind."

"I haven't changed my mind." I pause as I close and lock the door. "Did anyone see you coming here?"

"Why does it matter?"

"It doesn't really. But did anyone see you?"

He shakes his head. "No one was around."

Again, I'm relieved. Not because I'm ashamed of his spending the night, but because I don't want anyone to think of me as needy or horny or weak. I know it's not a rational feeling, but I still feel it.

I don't want anyone to know our business. This is just between Dave and me.

It feels a little awkward as we turn out the lights and get into bed. I'm brutally aware of Dave beside me, the feel of his shifting on the mattress, the sound of his breath, the smell of his soap and toothpaste.

I wonder what he's thinking about me.

"Are you okay?" His voice is low and slightly gravelly in the darkened room. "I know you've had a hard day, and I don't want to make it harder for you by pressuring you into something you're not comfortable with."

"I am—" I break off the words, since I don't want to lie to him. "I'm a little uncomfortable, but it's not because I don't want to be with you. It's just been a long time since I've . . . I've spent the night with anyone."

"I'm not going to do anything," he says, reaching out until he finds my hand and then holding it under the covers. "Except hold you, if you'll let me."

"I'd like that," I admit.

He leans forward, and I move toward him, and then we're kissing—nothing serious, just light and soft. He wraps his arms around me afterward, and I nestle against him.

It feels really good to just lie with him this way. I've forgotten how nice it is to lie with a man under the covers, just touching, just being together.

But I can't stay on this side. My hip simply won't allow it. So eventually I have to pull away when the discomfort becomes too strong.

"I'm sorry," I say. "I'm not pushing you away. But I have to turn over on my other side."

I feel him smiling in the dark. "That's fine. I can hold you that way too."

I realize what he means when I turn over and he spoons me. This is much more comfortable, and I spend a few minutes just enjoying it, processing how I want to be close to his man—physically and in every other way, how much his presence has helped me start to recover from yesterday.

"Can you sleep?" he murmurs, leaning forward to kiss my neck.

"I think so. What about you?"

"I can too."

"Good. Thank you—for everything, I mean."

I can hear the smile in his voice again. "You're welcome. Good night, Eleanor."

It's not long until I'm asleep.

I wake up several times during the night. I always do, since I have to pee every few hours. Whenever I wake up, Dave has rolled over, away from me, probably an automatic impulse in his sleep. But when I get back to the bed, he murmurs sleepily, "You okay?"

"Yes," I tell him each time. "I'm fine."

He reaches out for me then, and I let him, since his touch feels natural in the dark.

When I wake up at four, I'm alert enough to get up for real, but I don't feel like it quite yet. Instead, I wash my face and brush my teeth and go back to bed.

Dave's eyes are open, which I can see since I left the light on in the bathroom. "Are you getting up?"

"Not yet." I crawl under the covers and sigh with pleasure as he rolls over and spoons me from behind.

His hand gently rubs my stomach. "You feel good."

"So do you."

He likes that I said that. I can feel the pleasure. It makes me feel a little fluttery, that a few words from me can have that kind of effect on him.

I'm not used to this. I'm not used to any of this. And I'm not used to not knowing what to do.

I close my eyes and relax in his arms, and I must doze off for a while, since things feel a little different when I'm aware of my surroundings again.

Dave is still holding me, and I can feel his warm breath against my hair.

"Are you okay?" he asks, when I blink a few times and look over my shoulder at him.

"Yeah. I'm good." I stretch my legs and smile. "Thanks for staying with me last night. I . . . I needed you."

He adjusts enough to kiss me. "I needed you too."

He doesn't pull out of the kiss as quickly as normal, and I have to roll over so I can really get into it, sliding my hands into his hair and softening my body against his.

I feel warm and more fluttery than ever when he pulls away. He strokes my face with his knuckles. "Did you want to get up?"

"Not yet." I pull him down into another kiss, since I really enjoyed the last one.

His body is tenser than normal, and his mouth and his hands feel unusually urgent. The kiss becomes very deep, his tongue sliding eagerly against mine.

I'm gasping when he finally pulls away, and my hands are clutching at his shoulders.

"Eleanor," he murmurs thickly, leaning down to

press brief kisses against my jaw, my cheekbone, my throat. "You're so beautiful."

I laugh softly. I can't help it. "Don't exaggerate."

"I'm not. I think you're so beautiful. I always have."

His words take root in my heart, and I arch up slightly, say breathily, "Thank you."

Then he's kissing me again, in a way he's never kissed me before. It's passionate, so deep.

My body doesn't respond the way it used to when I was younger. It's much slower to react, the physical urges not nearly so intense. But they're growing slowly, and I know how to recognize the wash of heat, the pulsing pleasure.

I can't believe I'm feeling like this. I never thought I would again.

"Dave," I gasp, when the kiss, the sensations, the whole situation becomes overwhelming. "Dave."

He must hear something in my voice, since he pulls back, holding himself above me. His eyes are hungry, tender. "Is this not what you want, Eleanor?"

"I want to be close to you," I say, trying to think clearly.

"I want to be close to you too. In every way. But we'll only do what you're comfortable with."

"I . . . I don't know." I shift restlessly, hoping I'm not hurting his feelings. "I haven't . . . I haven't really thought about this. At our age, I mean."

"It happens."

"I know it does."

"We're not dead yet."

"I know we're not."

"We can go as slow as you want."

I take a shaky breath. "Thank you."

"Do you want me to get up?"

I shake my head. "Not yet."

He smiles and leans down to kiss me, softly this time. And I realize I want to feel like I was feeling before, so I hold his head down and open my lips, deepening the kiss.

He makes a rough sound in his throat, and his hands start to move over my body. He's supporting himself on his side, only his head over mine, leaving one of his hands free to trace the line of my breasts, my belly, my hips—over the fabric of my gown.

It feels really nice. I like to be touched like this, as if every part of me is beautiful, is worthy of being touched.

When his fingers twirl over my nipple, the thin material of my gown adding a new layer of sensation, I give a little jerk and make a silly, breathless sound.

He pauses, lifting his head to look at my face. "What was that?"

"Just a sound. What do you think?"

"I think I want to hear you make it again." His smile is teasing, but his fingers return to my breast, tweaking my nipple until I make the sound again.

He's chuckling as he kisses me, and he keeps fondling me at the same time. My heart is racing, my skin flushed, something like joy overflowing in my heart.

I'm touching him all over too, my hands skating over his arms, his back, his thighs. I can't seem to stop myself.

"You feel so good," he murmurs. He's managed to slip his hand under my nightgown, and now he's cupping one of my breasts and then sliding his hand down my side. I'm not particularly slim, and my skin isn't particularly smooth, but he doesn't seem to care. "I love how you feel."

"Dave." I feel so good in so many ways, but I'm starting to get nervous again. "Dave, I'm not sure I'm ready for . . . for intercourse."

Psychologically ready—maybe. Physically ready—maybe not. There are physical issues that need to be addressed when having sex at our age, and I'll feel better if I go to see a doctor about it first.

"Okay," he says, still pressing kisses against my skin. "That's okay."

I feel his reluctance, but he starts to pull away. I stop him by grabbing his shoulders. "But I don't want to stop."

I slide my hand down his T-shirt until I reach his waistband, then slip my hand beneath it. I explore until I find his shaft. He's partway erect but not completely. I stroke him between my fingers and thumbs.

He sucks in a breath in response. "Are you . . . are you . . . sure?"

"Oh, yes."

I keep caressing him, and soon he rolls onto his back, evidently too affected to hold himself up on his side. His face is twisting in pleasure, and I love the sight of it. I love that I can please him this much.

"Eleanor." His eyes are deep and intense, and they never leave my face. "Eleanor."

I love the sound of his saying my name. I used to be pretty good at a hand job, and I think I can still remember the basic skills. I feel his penis harden more, although slowly.

Then he suddenly pulls me toward him so we're kissing as I work him over. He's grunting against my mouth and then suddenly he's coming.

He didn't last long. He never got fully erect. And I don't really care. He's gasping with pleasure and falling back against the mattress, his expression relaxed and replete.

He's breathing so heavily and seems so overwhelmed that I ask after a minute, "Are you okay?" I pull my hand out of his pants.

"Yeah. Oh, yeah." He smiles at me. "Thank you."

I smile back. "You're welcome."

I nestle against him and let him recover, and after a few minutes, he's kissing me again and stroking my back.

"Do you want to try?" he asks. "I want you to enjoy this too."

"I am enjoying it. You have no idea how much."

His hand slips back under my gown. "Maybe you can enjoy it even more."

I don't actually know if this is true, but there's no reason not to let him try. I love how it feels when he kisses me. And when his mouth moves lower, to nuzzle my breasts, it feels just as good. And when he caresses me over my underwear, it still feels good.

Deep and warm and slow and good.

I'm breathing deeply, unevenly, and I'm making more of those silly noises that clearly feed his ego. My joints are aching but not enough to get in the way of the pleasure.

I'm starting to think we might actually have some success when the phone rings.

It's so surprising and so out of context that I don't immediately recognize it, but it keeps ringing until it pierces the haze in my mind.

"What the hell?" Dave grumbles.

That's about how I feel too, but I check the caller to see that it's one of the staff phones. It's just after seven in the morning.

"I better get it," I say, pulling away from Dave slightly. "It might be important."

The caller is Charlotte. "I'm so sorry," she says. "I hope you weren't still sleeping."

"No. I wasn't. What's the matter?"

"We're having some trouble finding Dave. Do you know where he is?"

I feel a weird clench in my stomach. "What?"

"Dave. I guess Kevin has been trying to call him and can't reach him, so he came over, but Dave isn't in his room. Do you happen to know—"

"He's here," I say, since there's no way to deny it. "He's with me."

"Oh, good," Charlotte says, not sounding the slightest bit surprised or disapproving. "That's a relief. Kevin is here now, and he'd like to see him, if that's possible. Do you think . . ." She trails off.

I glance over at Dave. "Kevin was evidently worried, so he rushed over here to make sure you're all right. He wants to see you."

Dave makes a face.

"I can tell him no," I say, almost hoping that's what he'll decide. I hate the way the call has interrupted such a private, intimate time between us.

Dave groans. "No. I better see him, or he'll be a pain."

"Well, if you don't want to talk to him now—"

Dave is already rolling out of bed. "It's not worth the trouble."

Okay. Well, there's that.

I tell Charlotte that Dave can see Kevin, and then I get out of bed myself, stretching the tension out of my muscles and pulling on my robe.

I'm going to look in the mirror to make sure I'm presentable when there's a knock at the door.

That was quick.

I open the door, and Charlotte is there looking

sheepish, with Kevin just behind her. He's frowning. I can tell he doesn't like the idea of my having spent the night with his stepfather.

I want to shake the disapproving look off his face, but that's obviously not something I'm allowed to do.

Dave is beside me, and he gives me a quick kiss before he walks out into the hall where Kevin is.

Charlotte says softly, "I'm sorry about this."

"It's fine. And it's not your fault."

I look over to Dave, but he's walking away with Kevin.

The whole thing feels different now. Not special and private and intimate. Kind of tawdry and awkward.

It's not rational that the whole thing should change in my mind that way, but it has.

I get dressed and manage to get to the dining room in time to have some breakfast. I sit with Gordon, who is as friendly and solid as always.

I don't enjoy my toast, fruit, and yogurt, though. I keep wondering where Dave is. Everyone who passes by my table asks, and I have no real answer for them, other than the fact that his stepson came by.

I hope that Kevin isn't being too nasty to Dave. I wish he would just go away and leave him alone.

A bad family isn't better than no family at all.

I'm returning to my room when Dave calls, asking if I want to walk. On cooler days, we've been walking in the late morning anyway, so I agree.

The sky is starting to clear, and it's becoming a decent day.

Dave looks kind of distracted when I join him. He kisses me, but only in a quick, unfocused way—like it's just a gesture. He's never kissed me like that before, and I don't like it.

It's not that I believe I always have to have his devoted attention. I'd just rather him only kiss me when he means it.

I ask him if everything is all right, and he gives a noncommittal answer that concerns me. I don't press him, though, and we walk in silence until we reach the bench.

Wet, dead leaves are covering the sides of the path, and they strike me as incredibly depressing. Just a few days ago, those leaves were vibrant with color on the trees.

"What did Kevin want?" I finally ask when we've situated ourselves on the bench. The sun is high in the sky now, and the warmth feels good on my face.

"He called several times last night and thought something had happened, so he rushed over this morning when he still couldn't reach me." Dave's face shows no expression, but I know he doesn't like for people to see him this way—as someone unable to stand on his own.

I don't like it either. I guess there are some people who like to be coddled, but for the rest of us growing old is a constant fight for self-sufficiency, to be like we were before.

"Maybe he was worried."

The nastier part of my brain wonders if maybe he was hoping that something serious had happened and Dave was on his way out.

I try to smother that side of myself. I don't like her.

"I guess."

"What's the matter?" I ask after another minute. Dave isn't looking at me, and he hasn't tried to touch me, so I know something is wrong. That isn't like him at all.

He shakes his head.

"Why can't you tell me?"

When he still doesn't answer, I frown at him. "Didn't we have a discussion yesterday about how we're together now, and so holding out on each other isn't right?"

He turns his head now and meets my eyes, reluctantly. "He's moving—out to Virginia Beach, where the rest of the family is."

I know it's unworthy, but my very first reaction is pleasure, relief. "Oh. Wow. When is he moving?"

Poor Charlotte will be crushed, but maybe it will be better for her in the long run.

"Next month." Dave clears his throat. "He wants me to move too."

"What?"

Dave looks away. "He does."

"He expects you to move all the way out there? Why? Why would you do that?"

"So I can be close to the family. Everyone will be out there then."

"But that's ridiculous. You're settled here. You're happy here, aren't you?"

He's looking at me again, his expression slightly cool, as if he doesn't appreciate the question. "Of course I'm happy here."

I can suddenly see that he might do it—no matter how much he'd prefer to stay. He doesn't put up a fight, not with his family. He's resigned himself to letting them walk all over him because he's so afraid of having no family at all.

He's going to do it. I can see it all now, with that clear sense of the future I sometimes get, grown sharper with age and experience. "Then why would you think about leaving?"

"What makes you think I am?"

"It sounds like you're considering it."

Naturally, I'm thinking about me. How sad and lonely I'll be if he leaves. But I'm also thinking about him. He won't be happy there—not the way he's happy here.

"Of course I'm considering it. I just haven't made a decision yet." He sounds grumpy now, and he's frowning down at the path, where a few wet leaves are scattered. "It would be nice to get some support."

So now I'm sad and scared and angry too—angry that he's whining about my not fussing over him when it feels like my whole life is about to fall apart. "Well, I'm sorry. I'm not going to support you if you're just going to let those stepchildren take advantage of you like that."

"What do you mean, take advantage of me?" His shoulders have stiffened in a way that doesn't bode well.

"They take advantage of you. They bully you around and expect you to give them money. They probably only want you out there so you can spend more money on them while you're alive."

The words are bitter, and I know I shouldn't say them. I know it. I can clearly see what Dave's reaction will be—I've known it all along, which is why I've been holding my tongue.

But sometimes you think a thing so often that eventually it has to be said.

He stands up abruptly, glaring down at me with a coldness I've never seen in him before. Then he just walks away.

Of course he's angry with me. I understand exactly why he is, even though I'm convinced my words were fairly accurate.

Accuracy doesn't always matter. I've just attacked

his pride and his judgment and the closest thing he has to a family—all at once.

He might not put up a fight, but he's not going to sit next to me after I do it.

twelve

*S*ometimes arguments are minor things that are forgotten the moment they're over, but sometimes they aren't.

Sometimes they last a lot longer than they should.

I sit on the bench for a long time, stewing over Dave and Kevin and the whole situation. Then I start to feel bad about what I said, so I stop by Dave's room to apologize.

He's not there. A nurse coming out of the next room tells me that Dave went on the day trip to a nearby waterfall, which left a few minutes ago.

Well, fine. If that's the way he wants to be, then I'll just give him some space. It's not like I want to hang around him constantly anyway.

I wish Marjorie were still here. I suddenly miss her like crazy. Feeling glum and restless and sad, I call up Beth, who invites me to have lunch with her. She's getting a manicure afterward, and she takes me along.

I feel better after lunch and a manicure. Dave will be back after dinner, and then everything will be fine.

Except Dave doesn't pick up the phone when I call him in the evening.

He's pouting.

I decide I've made enough efforts for the day. If he wants to be an adult about it, he can contact me. I go to bed and read until I'm tired. Then I fall asleep.

I can't help but think about how Dave shared the bed with me last night. I can't help but think about the way we were together this morning.

But I know how life works. It's always been the same. Never let yourself think daydreams are coming true, because the real world will just catch up with you—usually come crashing down around your head.

I don't sleep very well, and I wake up early. At least the sky is clear as I wrap up warmly so I can sit on my patio drinking tea and watch as the sky starts to lighten.

When it's light enough, I decide that there's just enough time to make it to the bench and back. I was taking walks in the mornings long before Dave came around. I'm not going to change everything just because he's angry with me.

Feeling determined, I get dressed, putting on a jacket because the air is still nippy. It will be lovely this afternoon, with the cool air and warm sun, but the sun isn't high enough yet to do much warming.

When I get in sight of the bench, I stop abruptly.

Dave is sitting there.

I'm tempted to turn around and go back, but that's a silly, petty gesture. I try very hard not to give in to such impulses. I don't always succeed, but I try.

I walk slowly over to the bench and sit down.

Dave has been watching me since I got into sight. I can't tell from his face how he's feeling this morning.

"I didn't think you were coming," he says at last.

"I always come."

He nods, his face softening just slightly.

It's enough. I was the one who said something wrong, so I'm the one who should apologize. "I'm sorry. For saying that yesterday. It wasn't nice, and it wasn't fair. I'm sorry."

He lets out a breath, and it looks like the tension is blown out of his body with his exhale. He reaches out to pull me against his side, wrapping his arm around me. "I'm sorry too, sweetheart."

He's never called me that before. He's never called me any sort of endearment. I like it.

I like it a lot.

"What are you sorry for?" I place my hand on his chest, over his heart. He's wearing a lot of clothes— T-shirt, sweater, jacket—but I can still feel his heartbeat on my palm.

"For being an ass about it."

I smile, and he wraps both arms around me in a hug.

I hug him back, feeling safe and secure and happy in his embrace.

He might not be as strong as he used to be, but he's strong enough for me.

I hope I'm strong enough for him too.

"Let's not fight anymore," I say, pulling away enough to look up at his face.

He's smiling, as if he's feeling something similar. "Agreed."

I'm not sure that I should ask the question right now, since it will bring back up a difficult subject, but I really need to know. "So what are you going to do about Kevin?"

He makes a face. "I don't know."

"Is he really pressuring you?"

"Not really."

I don't know if this is true or not, but I don't question it at the moment. "I'd hate for you to leave," I say, feeling rather vulnerable as I say the words, but saying them anyway.

His eyes are very tender on my face. "I'm not going to leave you, sweetheart. Surely you know that. I love you."

My breath hitches in my throat, and it takes me a minute to process that he's actually said what I think he's said. "You do?"

"Of course. Didn't you know that?"

"No. I didn't know that."

"Well, I do. I love you." He's still holding my eyes, and his expression has become questioning, expectant.

"I love you too," I blurt out, since I know it's true and I know I need to say it.

His face relaxes palpably. "Well, good."

"It is good."

"I agree."

So we're back to saying silly things, but I figure it's all right. He kisses me, slow and soft, and then he adjusts us so both of his arms can hold me comfortably.

He said he's not going to leave me. That's more of a relief than I deserve.

We sit together for a long time, the sun finally starting to warm up the air, the trees, the world.

Then I say absently, "I had a terrible night."

"So did I. I hardly slept at all."

"You should rest this afternoon," I say, thinking that he does look rather tired.

I don't like him to look tired. I don't like him to look anything but healthy.

I'm suddenly terrified that he's over seventy-five and doesn't necessarily have a lot of years to live.

The same is true of me, of course, but that doesn't bother me nearly so much.

"I'll rest," he murmurs, stroking my hair, "if you rest with me."

"Okay." I smile, staring out at Valentine Valley.

We do rest together that afternoon—in my bed. We actually do take a nap, followed by some leisurely kissing and caressing.

We both have a very nice time.

I make an appointment with the doctor for two days later.

I want to have sex with Dave if it's a possibility for us, but I'm worried about it being uncomfortable for me. Maybe some lubricant is all I need, but I'll feel better about getting some medical advice first.

I'm half excited and half embarrassed when I return with lubricant, a prescribed cream, and some good advice.

It's not like I'm going to jump Dave now that I have the necessary provisions. But at least it feels like it's a possibility.

Dave has asked me to go with him to the symphony on Friday night, so maybe that will be a good time for us to progress.

It's a strange week. Sometimes I feel a bit like a teenager, all jittery and excited about something that feels entirely new. In general, our routine this week is what it always has been. We walk in the mornings —after breakfast now because it's getting cooler— have our meals at normal times, and do some of the planned activities. It's not like I'm thinking about sex every minute of the day. That would be far too exhausting for me. But it does feel like I have a little secret that makes the everyday routine more exciting.

I do make a point of not having a lot of overblown fantasies. I've always been realistic, and I'm quite sure, when we finally get to do it, it's not going to be perfect.

And that's just fine for me. He loves me. I love him.

I never thought I'd be in this situation at my stage of life.

On Friday evening, I spend a lot of time showering and dressing before we leave. I wear a black satin skirt and a silk top that drapes nicely over my curves. I wear my best string of beads—gold alternating with lovely ruby-colored stones.

I just know tonight is going to be wonderful.

He comes to my door at exactly six thirty, wearing a black suit that makes him look very distinguished. He has a bouquet of roses for me.

I'm feeling quite giddy and am trying to talk myself down from it as we leave the residence, driven in a Town Car he hired for the occasion.

We go out to dinner first, and then we have excellent seats for the symphony. I know he must have spent a lot of money on this outing, and fortunately both of us seem to be enjoying it a lot.

It's late when we get back, and I'm feeling very tired. I never stay out this late, and I can barely keep my eyes open on the drive back.

But I don't want the evening to end yet. He's made such an effort tonight. I can make an effort too. I want to be with him in every way.

He leans down to kiss me at my door, and I wrap my arms around him. "Are you tired?" he murmurs against my lips.

"A little," I admit, not wanting to completely lie

to him. "Do you want to come in for a cup of tea or anything?" Maybe tea will revive me enough for us to progress to the rest of the night.

"Sure." He smiles and follows me inside.

The tea helps a little, but not much. And soon I'm trailing off whenever I try to say something to him.

"You're exhausted," he says at last, straightening up and looking at me fondly. "You should go to bed."

"Oh. Did you . . . did you want to spend the night with me?"

He pauses for a few seconds. "Are you sure?"

"I am. I really want to spend the night with you."

This seems to really please him, and I'm feeling both happy and sleepy as he leaves for a few minutes to go to his room to get ready for bed.

He comes back with a zippered pouch, which he tells me is his toothbrush and his medication for the morning.

This makes perfect sense to me.

I've changed into a pretty dark red nightgown, and I take off my robe rather shyly, aware that he's watching me.

The night seems very silent, the room very dark when we turn out the lights.

He pulls me into his arms, and we kiss for a minute. It's lovely, but I just can't concentrate.

"You're too tired," he murmurs, after he pulls away. His face is close to mine in the darkness.

"I'm sorry. I'm just not used to such late nights."

"I know. Let's go to sleep."

"I'm sorry."

"Don't be sorry. To tell you the truth, I'm tired too."

There's a dry note in his tone that proves he's telling the truth. I laugh softly and give him a hug. Then I turn over onto my side and he spoons me from behind.

It's very nice to fall asleep like this, to know that he's loving me, even as we drift off.

And I figure it's okay to not have had a steamy evening, even though I thought it would be.

There's always tomorrow, after all.

The next morning, I wake up aware that Dave has gotten out of the bed. A quick glance at the clock shows it's almost five.

I'm usually up before now. I did wake up a couple of times during the night to go to the bathroom, but that's normal and I fell right back to sleep.

I feel rested now, and I would feel comfortable if I didn't have to pee.

I hear the toilet flush and the water running from the bathroom. And then after a few minutes, Dave comes back into the room and crawls into bed beside me. It smells like he's brushed his teeth.

I get up immediately, since now I really have to go. I brush my teeth too, and then I brush my hair before I go back to bed.

He's awake. I can see his eyes open since I leave the bathroom light on like last time.

It casts a pleasing glow into the room—dim but not dark.

"How do you feel this morning?" he asks as I crawl back under the covers and roll over so I'm facing him.

"Pretty good. How about you?"

"I feel great."

"Good." Smiling, I scoot over so I can brush my fingers over his face. "I always have more energy in the mornings."

"Me too." He reaches out to kiss me, and we both know what we want, so it gets deep quicker than usual. Soon he has me rolled over onto my back. He's on his side, leaning over enough to keep kissing me.

"I went to the doctor earlier this week," I say rather breathlessly as his hand runs up and down my body.

"I know."

There's a particular timbre to his voice that I recognize. "But you don't know what I asked her."

"I might have an idea."

I gasp slightly and pull out of the kiss. "You do?"

"I know how to put two and two together." He's smiling now, and I love the mingling of humor and fondness, teasing and deep understanding I see in his expression.

I give an exaggerated sniff. "If you're going to be smug about it, then maybe I don't want to do anything about my doctor's appointment."

He chuckles and leans back down to kiss me. "I think maybe you do."

That kind of ego shouldn't be rewarded, but I'm too full of affection to put up much of a fight. I soften into the kiss, and our tongues start to glide together deliciously.

He's fondling one of my breasts. It all feels really good.

He seems to be taking his time, and I start to worry that he thinks I need a lot of coddling in order to get into the mood. So I say, "I'm good, Dave. You can start any time."

"I have started."

"I meant—"

"I know what you meant. But we're going to take care of you first."

I feel a little shiver of excitement, but I say, "Oh, you don't have to—"

"I know I don't have to." He raises his head with a wry look. "The truth is, I need to wait thirty to sixty minutes anyway."

My breath catches in my throat as I realize what he means. My eyes go wide. "You took a pill!"

He looks adorably sheepish. "I may have done."

I'm laughing as I hug him. "You didn't have to do that."

"I know. But I talked to the PA a few days ago, and she says it could help, if I'm worried. I just want to make sure it's good for you."

I'm so full of such a mingling of feeling that I can hardly contain it. "It's always good."

"I'm glad. But I've been kind of wanting to try it, anyway."

"Okay. We'll try it."

"So I might as well kill a little time in the meantime." He's smiling again, evidently relieved by my reaction.

That sounds like a perfectly reasonable idea to me.

He seems determined to bring me pleasure this morning, and he spends a lot of time kissing and caressing me. I enjoy all of it, my body buzzing pleasantly in response. I don't know if I can reach orgasm, though. It's not something that happens to me much anymore. I know he wants me to, and I don't want to disappoint him, but my body isn't what it used to be.

When Dave pushes up my nightgown and slides down my underwear, I feel a little anxious. I enjoy being intimate with him, but this is different—this is more.

To hide the anxiety, I reach over and pull the lubricant out of the nightstand drawer. "Here. The doctor suggested I use this."

Dave seems to think this is a good idea, as he squeezes some out onto his hands before he starts to stroke between my legs.

I'd been thinking he was ready to move on to his portion of events, but evidently not. He keeps stroking me as he leans down to suckle at one of my breasts.

Both at once feels very nice, and the additional moisture allows him to slide his fingers inside me. It's good. Really good. I breathe to stay relaxed. I'm not really expecting to come, but I might as well enjoy it. Even after a couple of minutes, he continues the ministration.

My pulse is quickening, though, and I'm so focused on breathing and staying relaxed that the orgasm hits me unexpectedly.

I cry out as the pleasure hits me, and I try to stifle it by turning my head into the pillow. But my body responds as it's made to respond, shaking and tightening and then relaxing deliciously.

Dave is smiling broadly as my mind starts to clear again and I stretch out with the kind of satisfaction I haven't felt in a really long time.

"Don't get smug," I tell him with a narrow-eyed look.

He laughs and pulls himself up so he can kiss me. "You didn't think I could do it."

"I never said so."

"But you were thinking it."

"Maybe. My body isn't what it was."

He shakes his head. "Your body is perfect."

"You're such a liar." Despite my words, I can't help but caress his face, his head, his shoulders. I want to touch him all over. I want to somehow express how full my heart is.

"It's not a lie if I believe it."

He means it. There's no way for me to deny it. With a throaty sound, I pull him down into a deep kiss.

As we kiss, he repositions himself so he's lying between my legs. He rocks against me lightly, and I can feel that his body has been responding too.

I reach down to stroke him, pleased and surprised to find that he's already much harder than I've felt him before. "I think that pill is working."

He groans in pleasure and rolls over, pushing down his pants so I can better reach his erection.

Both of our eyes widen as we see the effect the pill has had.

"Well, look at that," Dave says.

I burst into laughter at the awed note in his tone. Then he laughs too, and he rolls over to kiss me again. "I have condoms if you want to use one," he murmurs as he pulls away from my lips at last. "But I have a clean bill of health from the doctor."

"So do I. We'll be fine. Just . . . just be careful. It's been a really long time for me."

"It's been a long time for me too," he admits, reaching over for the lubricant again.

It's not nearly as scary as I thought it would be. He positions himself between my legs in a way that's basically comfortable for both of us, although he'll obviously have to do more of the work. The lubricant and my earlier orgasm have helped enough that it's not uncomfortable for me when he slowly maneuvers himself in.

We're both breathing heavily and looking each other in the eyes when he starts to rock slowly.

It feels good. And natural. And like we're loving each other. Even more so when he leans down to kiss me.

He doesn't move fast or hard, and the pill has helped enough that he can last a long time. There's no way I'm going to come again, but it feels really good, and I hear myself making silly huffs and sounds as we rock together. He's grunting too. We can't talk, but we don't need to talk. Anything we said would be irrelevant.

We're in this together, and both of us know it.

Eventually, his body starts to tighten more. He pulls out of the kiss and accelerates his breathing and his thrusts at the same time.

It's getting a little uncomfortable now for me as the lubricant starts to wear off, but not enough to make me want to stop. I love how he looks as he takes his pleasure in me, as he lets go of his restraint.

His whole body clenches and then releases as the pleasure spreads out on his face. I pull him down into a hug when he comes, breathing out my name and that he loves me.

I love him too.

More than I thought I could love anyone.

As we relax together afterward, I suddenly hate the fact that we no longer have a lifetime to spend together.

thirteen

*W*e spend a couple of hours in bed, relaxing and recovering.

Dave seems really pleased with himself, and it reminds me how much men look to their erections for their identities. He's been happy with me all this time. I know he has. Even without intercourse. But he's also really proud that he's been able to perform this way.

It's just after six now. We have plenty of time to dress and get to breakfast on time. I want to take a shower, and Dave does too, so we go our separate ways, planning to meet up before we go to the dining room.

I'm a little sore. My thigh and abdomen muscles are very tired. It's been a while since I've used them like that. But I feel good overall after I take a shower, and I'm looking forward to seeing Dave again.

Since he hasn't come to my door at five minutes to seven, I leave and walk over to his. I feel like I have a juicy secret as I greet the staff and residents I pass in the hall. I wonder if they have any idea about the kind of morning I've had.

I used to feel this way a lot—when I was young and had a particularly good sexual interlude. It's startling that I should feel the same way now, but the feeling is almost exactly the same.

Dave is just coming out of his door when I reach it.

"Sorry," he mumbles, checking to make sure his door is locked.

"It's fine. I was ready early, so I figured I'd save you the walk." I look at him closely. He's a little pale. "Are you feeling okay?"

He raises his eyebrows. "I'm fine."

"You look—I don't know—tired or something."

"I guess I could be a little tired." He gives me a secretive smile. "I don't know why I would be."

I smile back, feeling better. "We can take it easy this morning and get some rest."

We head to the dining room and take our normal table, where we're joined shortly by Gordon and another pleasant lady about my age named Veronica. Dave is quieter than normal as we eat, and he still looks a little pale to me, but he's probably just tired.

I'm tired too. I think I'll be taking a midmorning nap today.

Breakfast is relaxed. Dave gets up to get me a refill on my water glass. I've drunk the whole thing, feeling unusually thirsty. There are servers who go around and handle refills, but they aren't as ever-present as in a restaurant, and the drinks are always set up on the table against the wall near the kitchen.

I watch Dave as he walks back. I love the lines of his body and the shape of his face and the color of his eyes. But he's definitely looking pale this morning. Maybe he shouldn't have taken that pill.

As he nears the table, I see that his hand trembles slightly as it holds the glass of water.

I should have gotten up on my own to get more water. I shouldn't have let him do it for me, even though he offered before I even thought about it.

His hands don't usually shake.

As I'm having that thought, the glass of water falls out of his hand to crash to the floor and spill all over his shoes, the bottom of his pants, the carpet.

I'm about to make a gentle joke—since that helps when people are clumsy, as many of us are sometimes around here—but then Dave falls down too, next to the empty water glass.

He just slides to the floor.

There's a rush of noise, as several people jump up and a few women give little cries of surprise and distress.

I'm too shocked to do anything immediately.

Dave is lying there on the floor. He doesn't appear conscious. And my first thought is paralyzing: I'm sure he must be dead.

Dave isn't dead. There's no way I can express my relief when I realize this is so.

Two of the staff members run over to him, and the

nurse is summoned. They determine he is alive but unconscious, and the nurse says it looks like one of those episodes he had before.

It's not long before they declare him stable and get him on his way to the hospital.

Several people are fussing over me, and they're really getting on my nerves. I feel cold and rather stunned, but I'm not the one who just passed out like that. A few people encourage me to stay here and rest until I hear how Dave is doing and am able to go visit him.

That's the most ridiculous advice I've ever heard. I'm not so old that a scare like this will send me to my bed. And I'm not about to stay here when Dave is in the hospital.

So I drive my car over to the hospital by myself. The hospital is only ten minutes away, and I don't want anyone with me, fussing and getting on my nerves.

I ask about Dave at the front desk, and they direct me to a waiting area. I'm waiting there when Kevin comes in, looking hassled and urgent.

I'm about to get up and go over to speak to him when a nurse comes out and summons him back. He glances at me, and I'm sure he sees me, but he doesn't say anything.

So I wait some more.

When I see the nurse again, I go over and ask her about Dave. She looks sympathetic but says that, since I'm not family, I can't see him yet.

Back I go to sit down and wait.

It's terrible. After about an hour, every joint in my body aches, and there's no way I can get comfortable in the chair. Kevin hasn't made a reappearance. No one tells me anything.

If Dave is conscious, surely he'd be asking for me. But maybe he's still unconscious. Maybe he's slipped into a coma. Maybe he's already dead.

I'm shaking with nerves and emotions, and I can't help but wonder what I've done to myself—falling in love with someone when neither of us has very much longer to live. Whatever we have can't last very long. We're just setting ourselves up for pain.

It was so much easier before—when there was just me to worry about. I was alone, but at least I was secure and wouldn't have my heart torn out like this.

I've been waiting more than two hours when I finally see John Martin walking through the double doors and down the hall that leads past this waiting area. I jump up so quickly my hip catches, and I let out a little sound of pain.

He looks over, immediately recognizes me, and approaches.

"Are you all right?" His eyes study my face with professional efficiency.

"Yes. I'm fine. I've been waiting to hear news about Dave. Are you here to see him?"

"Yes, I was just with him." He frowns. "Has no one come to talk to you?"

"No. I'm not family, so they wouldn't let me back at first. I saw Kevin earlier, but . . ."

Dr. Martin shakes his head. "He left a little while ago, since Dave is stable. He's sleeping now."

I let out a breath of relief. "He's okay?"

"I think so. It's one of those episodes. He's had them periodically. It's something neurological, but we're having trouble pinning down what causes it and how to address it."

I take another deep breath. Then I say, a little hesitantly, "He . . . he took a pill this morning."

Dr. Martin's brows draw together. "A pill? What do you mean?"

There's no choice now but to admit it. "We were . . . intimate, and he took a pill. Do you think that could have—"

"Oh." Enlightenment has dawned on his face. He smiles at me kindly. "I don't think that would have done it. Who prescribed it?"

"The PA at Eagle's Rest. She seemed to think it would be fine for him."

"Yes, I'm sure it was." He looks down thoughtfully. "I'll make a note of it and check it out, but I really don't think that's what would have done it. He's had these before, you know."

"I know. I just . . . I was just worried."

"Of course you were." He glances back at the double doors. "He's stable now, so you can go back and sit with him if you like. He'll wake up in a little while, and I'm sure he'll be happy to have you there."

"Yes. Yes, thank you. I would like to do that."

I feel much better as I walk through the doors with him and down a hall to a private room. Dave is in the bed. He looks very old against the pillow and covers, surrounded by all the medical equipment.

My stomach churns as I sit down in the chair beside the bed.

"Can I get you anything? Maybe some tea? Or would you like something to eat?"

I'm about to refuse Dr. Martin's kind offer when I realize that it's late in the morning now, and I'm feeling quite weak. "Just tea would be wonderful. Thank you."

Dave is sleeping. I can see his chest rise and fall. One of his hands is resting outside the covers, and it looks very wrinkled and worn.

I hate this. I hate that he looks this way now, when he's always been so strong.

Dr. Martin returns with my tea and a pack of crackers and cheese, which I accept. Then he leaves, telling me he'll be back to look in on Dave later today.

So now I'm alone with him. I drink my tea and eat my crackers and wonder why I've done this to myself.

I would have been happier alone, without all this heartache.

He might not be dead right now, but he has something wrong with him that they can't diagnose and so they can't treat. It can't be good. Who knows how long he'll hold out? We can't even figure out things that trigger it, so there's no way to try to prevent the episodes.

I've been in the room more than an hour and have actually started to doze off when a motion on the bed brings me back to consciousness.

I open my eyes to see Dave shifting under the covers. As I watch, his eyes open.

After a moment, they rest on me. "Eleanor."

I make a foolish sound of emotion. "Hi. How are you feeling?"

"I . . . I don't know. What happened?"

"You had one of your episodes. You're in the hospital now."

He frowns, awareness and intelligence returning to his face, making such a drastic difference that it's almost shocking. "How long have you been sitting here?"

"Just an hour here," I say, not wanting him to know how long I had to wait before I was let into the room.

He looks to the tray table beside the bed. Seeing his watch, he lifts it up to peer at it. "You must have been here longer than that."

"I just got to the room an hour ago. I was in a waiting room before that."

"You've been here way too long. You need to go back."

"I do not. I need to stay with you."

He smiles tiredly. "I'm evidently just lying here."

"Does anything hurt?"

"My head, a little. Not too bad. Has Kevin been here?"

I try not to sneer at the name. "He was here earlier. He left once he found out you were stable and asleep. I'm sure he'll come by later."

"Yeah." Dave sighs. "You should go back."

"I'm not going to go back yet, and you shouldn't expect me to. I want to be here with you."

His face twists strangely, and he reaches out toward me. I assume he's looking for my hand, so I place it in his. He closes his cool fingers around mine and then raises my hand to his lips, pressing a kiss against the knuckles. "I'm sorry to worry you."

"What makes you think I was worried?" I'm deeply touched by the words and the little gesture. I'm feeling far too weak, far too scared.

I don't like feeling this way. I never have.

He gives a huff of laughter. "I know you, remember."

"I guess." I smile at him so he knows I'm teasing.

"I love you, remember."

"I do remember. I love you too."

"Good." He closes his eyes and lets loose of my hand. "I'm going to rest for a little while."

"Good plan."

I watch him as he falls asleep again, and I wonder if there's any possible way to protect my heart.

Life gives you things and then takes them away. If you're lucky, the giving and taking mostly balance out.

I stay with Dave most of the afternoon, but I'm so tired around supper time that everyone—the nurses, Dr. Martin, Dave—all insist I head back to the residence.

I know they're right, so I do it. I manage to eat a little bit, and I take a hot shower. Then I collapse on my bed and go right to sleep.

I wake up much later than usual—proof of how tired I was. The first thing I do is call Dave, and I'm pleased when he answers the phone. He sounds much more like his regular self. He tells me they'll probably keep him in the hospital today so they can run more tests, but he'll likely be able to come home tomorrow.

Then he tells me Kevin is coming to see him this morning, so I should take it easy and not come by until after lunch.

It makes sense. I don't really want to hang around if Kevin is there too. Plus, I'm still so tired I don't want to get out of bed.

So I have a leisurely morning, trying to talk myself

out of having a panic attack about being in a relationship with a man who might die at any time, and then I drive over to the hospital around noon.

I'm not going to let Dave see how I've been feeling. I don't want him to know how scared, how uncertain I suddenly am. My reaction is probably natural, but it's also unworthy. That's not—and never has been—how love is supposed to work. So I'll keep it to myself, and I'll work through it soon enough.

It's more important for Dave to know I love him and get better enough to come home.

He looks much healthier when I enter the room—at least physically. He's not as pale, and it appears someone has helped him with his hair, since it's not sticking out in all directions like it was yesterday.

I smile cheerfully and ask him how he's feeling. I'm surprised when he just mutters out a response.

I realize his expression is that grumpy one, when he's pulled back inside his shell.

"What's the matter?" I ask, sitting down next to him. I'd take his hand if he offered it to me, but he doesn't.

"Nothing. I mean, I don't know."

"Well, something is going on." My heart is starting to hammer—that tremor of warning that something bad is about to happen. I know it. I've lived long enough to recognize it when it comes. "Just tell me."

"Kevin wants me to move to Virginia Beach with him."

I sit up straight with a jerk. "I know. We talked about it before. You decided against it."

"I didn't really decide against it."

"Yes, you—" I stop myself, knowing arguing about something so trivial isn't worth the trouble. It doesn't matter whether he decided against it and is now changing his mind or if he never decided against it and just made me think he had. "Are you thinking about doing it?"

"I'm thinking about it. He makes a lot of sense."

"What kind of sense is he making?"

"Just that the whole family is there, and there will be a lot of people around to help me. I'm not getting any younger, you know."

Of course he's not. None of us are. And I realize that this episode has scared him too—just like it's scared me. This is his way of coping.

The realization hurts so much I can barely speak, but I manage to say, with a degree of my normal composure, "I thought you said you weren't going to leave me. You didn't mean that?"

"Of course I meant it." He's looking grumpy again, angry even. "How can you doubt it?"

"I doubt it because you're talking about leaving right now. What am I supposed to think?"

"Well, you can come with me." He scowls at me. "You can just come with me."

It feels like a slap in the face—an offer that's nothing more than an afterthought, an invitation so ludicrously impossible.

"Don't be ridiculous," I snap, tired of trying to sound calm.

"Why is it ridiculous?"

"Because I'm not going to leave. I've been here my whole life. This is where I want to be. You know that."

"Maybe I thought you loved me enough to let it go." He's muttering now and sounds bitter.

Probably about as bitter as I feel. "Right. I'm supposed to sacrifice everything because you can't say no to your stepchildren."

"That's not what this is about."

"Of course it is. You can't say no. You're too apathetic to put up a fight. And so you're willing to give up everything you have here to do what they want. And now you expect me to do the same thing when you're clearly prioritizing those spoiled brats who just take advantage of you over me. What? Am I supposed to find a new home there? What's that going to cost me every month?"

"I would—"

"Don't you dare offer to pay for me. You know better than that. I'm supposed to leave my family and everything I love here?"

"I thought you loved me." He's sulking now, like a child. I've seen old men do that over and over again when they don't get their way, and I'm tired of it. I'm tired of all of this. I'm supposed to be relaxing and taking it easy for my final years, and all I've had is angst and worry and frustration, and now this.

Heartbreak, I guess you could call it.

"This is not how love works." I stand up, since if I stay here any longer I'm going to cry.

He turns his head to glare at me coldly. "So that's it? You're giving up on us?"

"You've already given up on us. I'm just agreeing to your terms."

I turn and leave after that, knowing it's over, knowing it's hopeless, knowing I was foolish to ever think this could work.

We're not young anymore, investing in a long life together. There's not much left for us to even have, and the habits of a lifetime are simply too hard to break at this point.

I drive home and lock myself away in my room.

It's funny how something so small can shatter what two people have worked so hard to build.

I was part of a couple just an hour ago, and now I'm not.

Now I'm alone again.

When I was seven years old, I spent two weeks dreaming of a trip into town. Our parents had promised the trip to my sister and me. We were going to see a movie and go to an ice cream shop for milk shakes.

I was so excited about the trip. The anticipation filled my head for days. I slept in rag curlers the night before so my hair would fall in pretty curls. And, finally, on the afternoon, my sister and I got dressed up in our best ruffled dresses and patent leather buckle shoes.

We went to the movie first, and the whole family enjoyed it. Then we went to the ice cream shop for milk shakes. Sitting at the bar was a boy of about twelve. He wore a leather jacket and looked sour and rebellious. I'd seen boys like that before, and I didn't like them. I always gave them a wide berth.

I had to walk right past him to get to our table, though. I was holding my sister's hand. The boy was looking right at me, and so—being me—I stared right back at him.

Looking away would be a defeat, and I didn't like to be defeated even back then, even by mean boys of twelve.

As I passed, I heard the boy say under his breath, "Ugly cow."

I was sure he was talking about me.

I was seven, and the words just decimated me. I spent the whole time at the shop trying not to cry, trying to figure out if I was really ugly, why he would have said something like that to me. I felt so sick I could barely swallow my milk shake. My mother was sure I was ill, but the truth was I was just so upset.

People have sometimes thought that I'm unfeeling because I don't openly show what I feel. They think I'm not as emotional as more demonstrative people, that I don't feel things as deeply.

And they're so wrong.

That whole day was ruined for me—because of that boy's comment. Even the parts of it I enjoyed, that I spent so long looking forward to, were tainted for me.

I sometimes wonder if I could have talked myself out of it, and I wonder the same thing again now.

Because I'm feeling the same way as I go to bed— like I'm sick, like everything that's been so beautiful here at Eagle's Rest is now tainted, that I'll never get it back, like I'm still that little girl, devastated by one moment that changed everything.

I'm not a child anymore, however, and I tell myself it will be better tomorrow.

I hope it will be. Right now, hope is all I have.

fourteen

I wake up the next morning with a heavy feeling in my stomach. I sense it immediately, even before my mind catches up.

I've always hated that feeling—the sickening heaviness in your gut that's emotional but has a profound effect on your body.

I remember feeling the same way when I woke up after each of my little dogs died. I felt this way after Jeff and I broke up. I felt this way the morning after my mother died. It's like the night has blurred the acuteness of the grief temporarily, but your body won't ever let you forget that things are just not right with the world.

It takes me just a few seconds to remember that Dave and I have broken up. As I lie in bed, staring up at a mostly dark room, I keep picturing the rest of my days passing by, one by one, without him.

It's not a good vision of the future.

I manage to talk myself out of complete despair by reminding myself I've lived most of my life without him very happily.

If he's so selfish and spoiled that he thinks I'll do anything he wants, without discussion, purely for his own convenience, then there will be no way of living with him.

And if he's so resigned to letting himself be bullied that he won't even stand up for what will really make him happy—as both of us know staying here at Eagle's Rest will—then he'll never be able to make a real commitment to me.

It makes sense. We're both too old and used to our own routines to really change at this point, as you have to if you're going to start building a life with someone else. At this stage of life, it works better to just have someone to hang out with, rather than trying to make life changes based on a fantasy of love.

We're too old and wise for that. At least, I am.

I eat tea and crackers in my room rather than going to the dining hall for breakfast. I just don't have the energy to face everyone yet. They'll all be asking about Dave, and I'll have to somehow tell them that we're no longer together. There will be exaggerated sympathy and nosy questions and probably some secret pleasure at seeing us broken up.

People are like that. I'm like that sometimes. We're all, at heart, trying to fight our worst instincts and often not succeeding.

When it's light outside, I get dressed and go for a walk. It's a clear, sharp, dry day—my favorite kind of all. I make myself enjoy it, since there aren't that many days so nice in the year. The walk feels lonely and empty, but that's to be expected.

Each day, it will get better. I know it will. I've had plenty of experience to tell me that we slowly heal whether we want to or not. So I'm going to keep walking in the mornings to the bench, where I can look out on my beloved Valentine Valley. Dave isn't going to take that away from me.

I stay for about a half hour in a kind of numb state of resigned determination—if such a state of opposites can actually exist—and then I start to walk back.

Dave is supposed to get out of the hospital today. I hope he's had a good night. I hope he hasn't had a setback that would keep him in the hospital longer.

It will be harder when he returns to Eagle's Rest, but he'll be packing up and getting ready to move. We won't have to share the community much longer.

Then he'll be gone and I'll start again.

Sometimes, I try to look back over my life and count up the number of restarts I've had. I always come to the conclusion that there have been far too many to count.

As I'm walking back through the gardens, I see someone sitting under the arbor. In the spring, that seat must be beautiful, surrounded by fragrant blooms, but now it's kind of depressing, covered by nothing but dying vines.

It's Gladys, I see. Something is wrong with her. I can tell even from the distance. It's something about the way she's hunched over on the bench.

I walk to her, responding to an automatic spark of concern.

When I get close, I can see she's been crying. Her

eye makeup is running, and she's holding a crumpled wad of tissue. She's wearing her normal high heels and a bright green pantsuit, and her hair looks particularly brassy in the rising sun.

"Are you okay?" I ask.

She looks up, her face reflecting immediate embarrassment. Maybe I'm intruding, but you don't sit outside in a public garden and cry unless you secretly want someone to find you, comfort you.

She clears her throat. "I guess so."

That's invitation enough, so I sit down. Gladys and I have never been friends, but I know her. And you have to be pretty heartless to just walk away in such a situation.

"What's happened?"

She looks up at me. "My daughter is getting divorced."

Those five words and the fact that she's here crying about them tell me a lot about Gladys—a lot I didn't know before. "I'm sorry. Is it sudden?"

"Not really. She and her husband have had problems for the last year, but I thought they'd work through it."

"Was it nasty then?"

"I don't know. She makes it sound . . . more like she's finally just given up."

"That's really hard, but maybe it's best for her." I don't usually say things like that. They sound too easy, too simplistic for the real world. But I have to say something, and I can't think of anything else.

"Maybe. I know she hasn't been happy. I just thought . . ." Gladys sighs, and the streaks of mascara running down her cheeks strike me as incredibly sad. "I just thought they would make it through. Her father and I were married for fifty-one years."

"Wow." I hadn't known that about Gladys either. "That's amazing. You must have been very happy."

She shakes her head. "Not all the time. But I loved him."

I haven't expected anything to run this deep in Gladys, and that's my mistake, my judgmental nature, trying to sum up a whole person in high heels and bleached hair. "That must have been a beautiful relationship," I say, trying to say something of what I feel while still being encouraging.

"It was. I wanted that for Candice too."

"Maybe she'll still find it. Maybe it will just look different than yours did. Don't you think that's possible?"

She pauses for a minute, obviously thinking about these words. Then she nods. "Maybe. Maybe."

I sit with her for several more minutes, until she reaches over and pats my arm in a silent thank-you.

I don't really feel better when I return to my room, but at least I have something else to think about.

I discover another lost soul about an hour later, when Charlotte drops by my apartment to check on me.

I can tell something's wrong immediately, even through the cheerful smile she gives me. "Dave is coming back today, isn't he?" she asks.

She doesn't know we've broken up. There's no reason she would know, unless Dave told Kevin, who told her. But I suddenly realize why there's a brokenness under her smile.

Kevin is moving. She's had to finally admit to herself the hopelessness of their relationship.

It's a terrible feeling—finding out you've been emotionally investing in a lie. I know this from experience.

"That's what I heard." I step aside to let her in.

"Have you talked to him today?"

I try to decide whether I should just blurt out our breakup or save it until later, when it's obvious to the whole community. "No. I haven't."

"I guess there's no reason for you to go visit him this morning, since he'll be coming back later today."

"I'm not going to visit him."

Under normal circumstances, she would probably have noticed something in my blank replies, but she's too distracted by the feelings she's trying to keep under control. I can see the struggle on her full, even features, even as she's hiding her expression. "That makes sense," she says.

I want to know what she thinks about Kevin and the whole situation, so I say casually, "I hear that Kevin is moving."

She's been doing her normal thing of picking things up in the room—although the only thing for her to pick up is my tea cup. Her body grows very still as she stands over the sink. "He is."

"That must be hard."

Her face twists. "I should have expected it."

"Did he . . . did he promise anything?"

She shakes her head. "No. He never did. I just . . . I just thought it meant something."

Of course she did. That's what so many women do. Men will spend time with them, kiss them, have sex with them even—just because it's easy and they're there—and women will assume that the actions are a declaration of feelings.

When, in reality, they're nothing but actions.

"I know it's hard," I say, falling back on the same words I used with Gladys, "but maybe it's for the best."

She's not crying. She looks broken, though, like she's barely holding herself together. "I don't see how."

"Yeah, I know. It always feels that way. But it won't always feel that way."

"It's just hard when . . . when he might have been my last chance."

"That's just not true. You're young."

"I'm over forty."

"That's young, as far as I'm concerned. You still have plenty of time."

"I guess. But I want kids, you know."

I can't answer immediately, because that hurts. It hurts me, even secondhand. Love might be able to bloom at any age, but children can't. There's a time limit imposed by our bodies, and all the medical miracles in the world can't necessarily counteract it.

I sigh. "I'm sorry. But you never know what will happen."

She straightens up and smiles at me, as if she's willing herself to feel better. "I guess so. I mean, look at you and Dave, falling in love."

Right. Look at Dave and me. Proof that anything can happen.

"It's never easy," I say, and even I'm not sure whether I'm talking about her situation or about mine.

Maybe it's both. Maybe it's everything.

Deciding I'm going to do something good today, no matter how miserable I feel, I say, "I'm really sorry about Kevin, but I'm pretty sure there's someone else who is interested in you."

She looks genuinely surprised. She obviously has no idea. "What are you talking about?"

"You might spend some time noticing Dr. Martin."

There's the oddest succession of emotions on her

face—confusion, self-consciousness, resistance, embarrassment. "That's crazy."

"I don't think it's crazy. I see a lot, you know."

"I know you do." She stares at me for a minute. "But I'm not sure he's my type."

"I think that's because you've never really noticed him. It might be worth considering. I have good instincts."

She ducks her head. "Maybe."

I'm not fool enough to believe that I've fixed her with a little bit of matchmaking. She's still going to be hurt and sad about all the time she wasted with Kevin.

It's one thing to have something real and then lose it. It's another to realize you never had anything real.

I think about that a while as I sit in silence, staring out at the gardens and at the beginning of the path that winds around the woods and reaches a bench that looks onto the valley.

I wonder which is true of Dave and me.

Have I been fooling myself this whole time, believing that what we have is real?

Or have I had something real and then lost it?

I go to lunch, even though it will be safer and easier to just stay in my apartment.

I don't want to fall into depression, and I know the best way to avoid that is to get out and think about something else.

I see Gordon sitting by himself, having arrived at the dining room twenty minutes early as he always does, and I take a seat with him.

"How is Dave?" he asks.

I can't resent him for asking this. Everyone will, and it's perfectly understandable. Dave passed out on Sunday in a crowded room, so naturally the concern and curiosity about his health will be universal.

I'm the obvious person to ask. I'm supposed to be his partner.

"I think he's okay. The doctor believes it was just one of those episodes, and he should be back to normal pretty soon."

"Good. When does he get out the hospital?"

"Today, I think."

Gordon looks at me sharply. "Why don't you know?"

"I haven't talked to him since yesterday."

"Is everything all right between you?"

I shake my head and say lightly, "Not really."

Gordon sighs and stares down at his place setting. "I'm sorry to hear that."

"It's just one of those things. It's hard—at our age."

"Yeah. I guess."

"It's hard at any age," I add.

"Yes. It is."

"How did you and Wendy do it, starting a relation-ship so late in life?"

He gives me a curious look. "I don't know. The same way anyone else does it—with a lot of patience and trust. It was worth it, though. I just had her for a year, but it was worth it."

The words are poignant, and they make my throat close up. I can't say anything. Evidently I don't have to. Gordon is obviously in an introspective mood, and he looks around at the tables filled with seniors. "People get together a lot here. I watch them. Some-times it seems like they just get together because it's convenient, so they won't be bored and lonely. And sometimes it seems like they've been waiting for each other all their lives."

"Which were you and Wendy?"

He meets my eyes. "Both. Either. I don't know. I loved my wife for forty years, and then, after she died, I found Wendy. My life was complete before I found her, but it was even better afterward. Even now, after losing her, it's better than it was before."

"I guess," I say, trying to process the words. "I'm not really in the same situation. I didn't spend my life with someone. I spent most of it alone."

"But it was a good life?"

"Yes. I think so."

"Is it better with Dave—right now, I mean?"

"I . . . I don't know."

He tilts his head slightly and gives me a little smile. "I think maybe you do."

After lunch, I go back to my apartment and try to watch a British mystery and do a word game, but I can't really focus on either one.

I keep wondering if Dave is back, if Dave is going to move really soon, if he will want to talk to me at all—even just to say good-bye.

I hope he's feeling better.

I hope he's okay.

I hope he's missing me . . . at least a little.

I'm fighting a battle with my mind, trying to concentrate on anything but Dave, when my phone rings.

I see that it's Beth, so I pick it up.

"Hi, Aunt Ellie, how are you?"

She's a young woman with a career and an active social life. It's really sweet of her to remember me and make an effort to occasionally connect.

"I'm fine, dear. How are you?"

"I'm getting over this very annoying cold. Dad said your boyfriend was in the hospital."

"Oh. He was. I mean, he is." There's no reason to be taken aback by the conversation, but I am.

Beth sounds slightly amused. "Well, is he or isn't he?"

"He's getting out today. It's just that he's not my boyfriend anymore."

"What? Why not?"

"It's . . . just one of those things. He wants to move, so it just won't work out."

"I thought he loved it there as much as you do."

"He does. I think he does. But his family wants him to move."

"Oh. I'd think they'd be thinking more about him."

"Yeah." I let out a long breath, trying not to be so judgmental. "Well, maybe they are. Maybe they really think he'll be better off closer to them."

"But he has you here. Why would he be better off somewhere else?"

The words are as depressing as anything I've heard yet today. "I don't know. But he's going."

"I guess it's not possible for you to go with him."

"I don't want to move. I love it here."

"I know. I know you do." She speaks quickly, as if she's afraid she's offended me. "I was just thinking that, if you really want to be with him, it might be a possibility."

Of course it's a possibility. And I have to admit to myself that if Dave had asked me in a way that made me believe he understood what a sacrifice it would be, I might even have considered it.

Maybe. I don't really know.

"As you get older," I say slowly, "you get more and

more set in your ways. It's hard to just pick up and change. It's not like getting together with someone in your twenties, when both of you are really just forming your lives."

"Yeah. I guess so. It just makes me sad, though. You two seemed really good together."

I swallow so emotion doesn't sound in my voice. "Maybe we were."

"You don't think he'll stay for you?"

I'm not willing to move for him, so there's almost no chance that he'll be willing to stay for me. It's simply too much bending. We're no longer strong enough to bend without breaking.

"Probably not."

"I'm really sorry. Won't you be lonely when he goes?"

"At first, I'm sure I will. I'll miss him. But I'm used to being alone, and I've never minded it before."

"Okay. Well, as soon as I feel better, I'll come take you out to lunch. How will that be?"

"That would be lovely. Thank you."

"You're welcome." She pauses. Then says, "I've always thought that, once you're older, people get smarter and make fewer mistakes. But we don't, do we?"

I almost laugh. "No. We definitely don't."

I sit on my recliner for the rest of the afternoon.

Then finally, at about four o'clock, the compulsion to know if Dave is back and if he's really okay is simply too strong.

It doesn't matter if we're not a couple anymore. I want to make sure he's all right.

So I get up and walk down the hall, turning the corner toward where his apartment is. I hesitate briefly before I start to walk down.

I'm halfway down the hall when I see his door is open.

It probably means he's back. Maybe he just arrived.

Or maybe he's already packing up boxes and someone is carrying them to the car.

I've made it this far, so I have to continue. I have to know that everything is okay with him.

As I'm approaching, Charlotte walks out through his door and starts to shut it. Then she turns her head and sees me drawing near.

"Ellie," she says with a smile. "I was just checking on Dave. He just got back."

Well, that answers my question, doesn't it?

"Really? That's good. Is he feeling all right?" I keep my voice soft so it doesn't carry into his apartment. The door is still slightly cracked, since Charlotte paused with the knob in her hand.

"Yes. He's feeling much better. Why don't you check on him yourself?" She gives me a smile that's almost mischievous, and somehow I know she's starting to feel better about her own situation.

If she can feel better so quickly, then my suspicions are confirmed that she never actually loved Kevin. That's good. That's really good.

"I think he'd be very happy to see you," she adds, opening the door again.

I stop in my tracks, my mouth partway open, but no words come to my lips. Naturally, I should decline the suggestion. We made a clean break, and I'll just look like a fool if I try to hang around after everything has been said.

But I want to see him. And I'd like to think that I have gotten a little wiser as I've aged. Pride doesn't mean nearly as much as we all believe it does. Some things are far more important.

So I give Charlotte a little flicker of a smile and start through the door. I almost run right into Dr. Martin, who is on his way out.

"I'm so sorry," he says, with his kind smile. "I have a bad habit of almost knocking you over, don't I?"

I smile at him, and I see Charlotte smile too. And I feel a great wave of satisfaction as I watch them walk down the hall together.

It's not like they're a couple now—or anything close.

But at least Charlotte seems to have noticed the man.

He's a man who deserves to be noticed.

So now the door is still open, and Dave is inside.

I walk in, closing the door quietly behind me.

I take several steps before I see Dave. He's sitting in his big leather chair, looking out one of the large windows.

I clear my throat, so he'll know I'm here.

He gives a little jerk and turns around. He's wearing a T-shirt and track pants and white gym socks. He looks older than usual and so incredibly tired.

"Eleanor?" His voice is slightly hoarse.

"Yes. It's me. Is it all right for me to come in?"

His face transforms. "Of course it's all right."

fifteen

I come farther into his living room and stand awkwardly for a moment until I decide to sit down on the couch, perched on the edge of the cushion, in case he doesn't want me to stay for very long.

He's just staring at me now. For a moment, I thought I saw something like relief and awe on his face, but now it's blank, so I'm not sure if the expression I'm hoping for was really there or not.

It could be my imagination. Wishful thinking. It's been known to happen before.

"How are you feeling?" I ask at last, since someone needs to say something.

"Okay."

"You still don't look up to full strength." He doesn't. He looks a little pale, although better than he was yesterday, and there's a shakiness about him that I'm just not used to seeing.

It scares me. Makes me think of watching him get older and older, frailer and frailer.

"I'm not, but I guess I'll be feeling better soon. That's what they say, anyway."

He looks more resigned than usual, and I hate the sight of it. It's wrong. Dave Andrews just shouldn't look like he's given up. It's not who he really is.

"Did the tests come back with any results?"

He shakes his head. "Nothing definitive. They still don't know what's causing these episodes."

"So what did they say?"

"The same as they did before. We'll keep watching it, but there's nothing really to do unless it gets any worse."

That scares me too. Of course it does. "Do they think it will get worse?"

"They have no idea."

"So you have this neurological thing wrong that they can't do anything about?"

"Pretty much." He gives me a faint smile. "They say I'm in great health otherwise."

I shake my head, staring down at my lap. "How long do you go between episodes?"

"I've had four. The shortest length between them has been three months. The longest is seven."

"Did the one you just had come the soonest?"

"No. It's been almost five months since I had the last one, I think. It's been two and a half months since you, and the episode was a couple months before then."

I notice he's keeping time by the day he reconnected with me. I can't help but like that fact. I feel like everything has changed since he came back into my life, and maybe he feels the same way.

"At least they don't seem to be getting any closer together."

"Yeah. I guess."

We sit without speaking for a minute.

Finally, I say, "It's scary."

"What is?"

"This thing you have—something wrong with you that can't be identified or fixed."

"It happens."

"I know."

"Knowing what's wrong doesn't mean it can be fixed."

"I know."

He hesitates before he murmurs, "It is kind of scary."

And I know that's why he made the decision to move, even though it isn't really what he wants. I know he feels like he's not in control of his health, of his life, and so he wants the safety net of being close to family, people he can be sure will take care of him if he goes downhill.

If he stays here, he'll have the staff of Eagle's Rest, and he'll have me. But maybe that's not enough.

I wouldn't want to leave Roger and Beth. I can understand.

I clear my throat. "When do you move?"

"I don't know."

I look up to check his expression and notice he looks slightly uncertain. "When does Kevin leave?"

"Three weeks."

"I guess it would make sense for you to move at the same time."

"I suppose."

"Will you find another home to live in there, or are you planning to stay with one of them?"

"I don't know."

I feel the strangest sort of jittery excitement, even though there's absolutely no reason for it. It's difficult not to hope, even when there's no reason for it. "Why don't you know?"

"It's hard."

"Yeah. I'm sure it is. You've been here a long time, and you . . . well, I think you really love it here."

"I do love it here." He's suddenly meeting my eyes.

"But you really think leaving is the best option for you?"

"I don't know." He looks down and then up again. "What do you think?"

"You know what I think."

He lets out a breath. "I guess so."

There's a turmoil going on in my chest, and I'm having trouble keeping my hands still. I'm twisting them together on my lap, trying to channel the rising anxiety and excitement.

I have no idea why I feel this way. Nothing appears to have changed.

But maybe something has changed. Maybe it's me.

I've spent my life never being vulnerable, never showing fear or need. I've been that girl up in the tree, nearly falling to her death but determined not to let anyone know.

I could stay that girl. I could be the person I've always been. I could watch Dave leave and spend a quiet, peaceful life without him.

Or I could bend a little. I could reach out a hand.

"If it helps," I begin, the words breaking slightly in my throat, "I could . . ."

"You could what?" He straightens up, something sparking in his face that wasn't there the moment before.

"I could consider . . . moving with you. Talk about it, at least."

He stares at me motionless, his lips slightly parted.

This is not a response that makes it easier for me—this absolute shock. "I mean, you know I want to stay here, but I can at least check it out. Maybe we could find some place nice there. If . . . if . . ."

"If what?" he breathes, still not moving.

"If you really want me. With you."

He makes a choked sound and reaches out his hand. It fumbles for a moment before it finds and grasps mine. "If I really want you?"

"Yes." I feel self-conscious and kind of foolish and incredibly vulnerable, and I can't quite meet his eyes. I've never done anything like this before. Not once in all my life. "I wouldn't want to consider such a big step unless you really . . . I mean, unless we're really in this together."

He still doesn't speak. I can hear him breathing in the quiet room.

Then finally, he says, "You would leave here for me?"

"Well, maybe. I'd consider it, anyway. I'm not saying for sure, since I have to feel like the situation would really be good for both of us."

He takes my hand in both of his and holds it very tightly. "I love you, Eleanor."

I swallow hard. "I love you too."

"I don't want to do anything without you."

I'm shaking now—in relief and emotion, since I can hear the truth of it, see the truth of it, feel the truth of it, in his presence beside me. "Me either."

"And I don't really want to leave Eagle's Rest."

I make a brief little sobbing sound as the words hit my brain. "What?"

"I don't want to leave. It felt like . . . like it would be easier, if I just went with my family. They all seemed so sure of it, and I don't always . . . I don't always trust myself anymore. And when I thought you didn't really want to commit to me, then I decided it would be best just to leave. But I don't want to leave. I want to stay here with you. I'm sure of it."

My throat is tightening, and my eyes are burning. "You are?"

"Yes." He holds my eyes and raises my hand to his lips. "So will you stay here with me—for the rest of our lives?"

I nod through the emotion.

He kisses my knuckles again. "Is that a yes?"

"Y—yes!"

He moves from the chair to the couch so he can wrap me in his arms. I'm shaking, so I cling to him tightly, and I'm surprised that I don't feel weak.

Maybe that's the difference. If both of you bend, maybe neither one has to break.

When you're young, the first instinct after such a romantic, emotional moment might be to fall into bed and do some passionate, life-affirming lovemaking.

Dave and I take a walk.

We take the path around the woods until it reaches the bench, and then we sit down to gaze out on the valley. We don't talk very much. Dave still seems really tired. He's walking much slower than normal, as if his episode has taken a toll on the rest of his body. It worries me. Of course it does. But I don't coddle him, since I know that will make him feel worse.

He's better today than he was yesterday, and he'll probably be even better tomorrow.

I can hope, anyway. We can hope.

No matter what else I'm feeling, I mostly feel

incredibly happy, and I'm sure Dave does too. I can see it in his face, despite the fatigue, as he smiles over at me.

It's a cold afternoon. It's already November. The fall is almost over. The woods are half naked, gray and gnarly and chilled, but at least the sun is shining very brightly.

"I was thinking," he says at last.

"What about?"

He's holding my hand in both of his, stroking the back with his thumbs. "They have couples' apartments—in the residence, I mean," he says, that old, seductive charisma in his eyes. "They're very nice."

My heart does a little jump of excitement, but I say primly, "Do they? How interesting."

He chuckles and reaches over to pull me against him. "I think we could fit in one of those apartments very nicely."

"You do move fast, don't you?"

Leaning over to brush a kiss against my hair, he murmurs, "I've always been a fast mover, but I've also always known what I want. And what I want more than anything is you."

"You have me," I tell him, raising a hand to cup his face. "And we can definitely take a look at those couples' apartments."

He kisses me, and I know he's very pleased with my response.

I'm pleased with it too.

It's been decades since I've lived with another person, but I want to live with Dave. I want to be around him as much and for as long as I possibly can.

Plus, it will quickly get tedious trying to move back and forth between our places. I've always been practical, in addition to all my other characteristics.

We sit together, his arm around me, for a half hour or so. I find myself gazing at a branch of a nearby tree. It's thick and cracked with age, bent with awkward humps and dips, but there's something mesmerizing about it.

"Look at that," I say, after a while.

"The branch?"

"Yes."

"What about it?"

"Isn't it beautiful?"

I'm not looking at his face at the moment, but it sounds like he's arching his eyebrows in that skeptical way he has. "Beautiful isn't the first word I'd use."

"It is beautiful. Look at those few leaves that are still hanging onto it. Look how gorgeous and red they are against the bark." There are about five, and they're clinging resiliently, fluttering slightly in the breeze.

"The last few holdouts of the fall, I guess."

I can't help but smile. "Yes, that's exactly it. I wish I could take a picture."

Dave, being Dave, pulls out his phone from his jacket pocket and snaps several photos of the branch and the five red leaves.

"Thank you," I murmur, stretching up so I can press a kiss on the corner of his mouth.

"Anytime, sweetheart. Just say the word."

When we get back to my residence, I tell Dave that he needs to get some rest. With a whimsical smile, he says he'll take a nap if I take one with him.

I have absolutely no objection to this suggestion.

So we both get comfortable and lay down on my bed. He scoots over so he can spoon me from behind, and I feel safe and warm and loved.

He falls asleep within five minutes, and then he rolls back over in his sleep. I turn to watch him.

He doesn't snore, but he breathes heavily in his sleep. The sound is quite evident in the otherwise quiet room.

I wonder for a moment if it will get annoying. I'll be moving in with him, after all, so I'll be sleeping with him all the time. What will I think about hearing that breathing every night, all night? Will I get annoyed and have to wear earplugs? For so many years, I've been used to sleeping in perfect silence.

I watch and listen to him for a long time, and I finally conclude that it's really the wrong question.

Dave is so much more than the sound of his breathing while he sleeps. The sound is connected to an entire man, an intelligence, a sense of humor, a strong spirit, a kind heart, a human soul.

A man I love.

So I eventually fall asleep, listening to him breathe.

I wake up when he gets up to go to the bathroom. When he returns to the bed, I get up to go to the bathroom too.

He's waiting for me. He rolls over as soon as I get back into bed. He's smiling when kisses me, and I wrap both of my arms around him.

He kisses me and caresses me for a long time, and I do the same to him. It doesn't feel like we need to do anything else.

He's only two days out from his episode. He certainly doesn't need any strain right now. And I don't feel like anything that's not soft and tender. His hands on me, his lips on me, are more softly tender than anything I've ever experienced.

I never would have dreamed he could be this way, back when we both worked at the college and argued all the time.

There's a lot you don't know when you're young. There's a lot you don't know until you really love someone.

"Sweetheart," he murmurs, his lips against mine, his hand caressing one of my thighs.

"Hmm?" I've got both of my hands tangled in his hair, my fingertips running over his scalp.

"I love you."

"I love you too."

"I never dreamed I would have something like you waiting for me, this late in my life."

"I know. I feel the same way. It's like a miracle."

He lifts his head to look into my eyes. "Sometimes I wish I would have found you sooner, so we could have longer together."

"Me too. But then I decide I wouldn't have been ready for you then."

He thinks about this for a minute, in that way he has, and he nods. "Yeah. I think that's exactly right."

We end up lying together for most of the afternoon, sometimes dozing and sometimes touching, loving each other.

He might die tomorrow. Or a year from now. Or twenty years from now. It's impossible to know.

I might die tomorrow too.

It's not something we can know, and I'm not going to let it keep me from living what's left of my life with him.

After a while, I start to think that, for most of my life, I've been single, independent, and self-sufficient, and I've enjoyed being that person.

But that doesn't mean I have to be that same person for the entirety of my life. I can change and still be me.

People do it all the time.

I've always thought that being single is an essential part of who I am—like being a dog lover and a nature lover and a walker and a reader.

But maybe it doesn't have to be.

Right now, I'm starting to think it could even be possible that I marry this man one day.

He may not ask me, but he's an old-fashioned guy, and I think he probably will.

I'll probably say yes, if he does.

I don't know how long we'll be together, how many more autumns we'll see, but I know the time will be beautiful. And I can hope that it will be long.

I'm a human being, after all, and *hope* is what we do.

author's acknowledgments

Many thanks to Ruthie and Mary Ann, for proposing the idea for this book. I never would have written it otherwise.

about the author

Noelle Adams handwrote her first romance novel in a spiral-bound notebook when she was twelve, and she hasn't stopped writing since. She has lived in eight different states and currently resides in Virginia, where she reads any book she can get her hands on and offers tribute to a very spoiled cocker spaniel. She loves travel, art, history, and ice cream. After spending far too many years of her life in graduate school, she has decided to reorient her priorities and focus on writing contemporary romances.

credits

AUTHOR	Noelle Adams
COPYEDITOR	Annamarie Bellegante
COVER PHOTOGRAPHY	Jan Rios
COVER MODEL	Barbara Homrighaus
PHOTOGRAPHY ART DIRECTION	Samantha Novak
COVER DESIGN	Monika MacFarlane
PROOFREADER	Beaumont Hardy Editing
INTERIOR DESIGN	Williams Writing, Editing & Design

Brain Mill Press would like to acknowledge the support of the following Patrons:

Rhyll Biest

Katherine Bodsworth

Lea Franczak

Barry and Barbara Homrighaus

Kelly Lauer

Susan Lee

Sherri Marx

Aisling Murphy

Audra North

Molly O'Keefe

Virginia Parker

Cherri Porter

Erin Rathjen

Robin Drouin Tuch

Printed in Great Britain
by Amazon